NOTES FROM THE BLENDER

TRISH COOK AND BRENDAN HALPIN

EGMONT
USA

NEW YORK

EGMONT

We bring stories to life

First published by Egmont USA, 2011
443 Park Avenue South, Suite 806
New York, NY 10016

1 3 5 7 9 8 6 4 2

www.egmontusa.com
www.trishcook.com
www.brendanhalpin.com

Library of Congress Cataloging-in-Publication Data
Cook, Trish.
Notes from the blender / Trish Cook and Brendan Halpin. — 1st ed.
p. cm.
Summary: Two teenagers—a heavy-metal-music-loving boy who is still
mourning the death of his mother years earlier, and a beautiful, popular girl
whose parents divorced because her father is gay—try to negotiate the
complications of family and peer relationships as they get to know each other
after learning that their father and mother are marrying each other.
ISBN 978-1-60684-140-2 (Hardcover) — 978-1-60684-186-0 (eBook)
[1. Interpersonal relations—Fiction. 2. Dating (Social customs)—Fiction. 3.
Stepfamilies—Fiction. 4. Same-sex marriage—Fiction. 5. Homosexuality—
Fiction.] I. Halpin, Brendan II. Title.
PZ7.C773No 2010
[Fic]—dc22
2010011315

Book design by Room39b

Printed in the United States of America

CPSIA tracking label information:
Printed in March 2011 at Berryville Graphics, Berryville, Virginia

To Team Cook and all our awesome adventures
yet to come.
—T.C.

To the Halpin/Neslon/Demarco family.
I love being in the blender with you.
—B.H.

NOTES FROM THE BLENDER

CHAPTER ONE

DECLAN

AUNT SARAH SAT IN HER PRIUS UNTIL I ACTUALLY opened the door to my house. Sometimes I like this—it's a stupid little gesture that helps me feel like I'm cared for. Other times— like that afternoon—I find it kind of annoying. I mean, I'm six-teen years old. I've had my own key to this house for seven years, and it's not like Dad's going to change the locks.

Still, Aunt Sarah didn't drive off until I actually turned my key in the lock and waved at her.

I could tell something was wrong as soon as I walked in the door. Dad was wearing his we-need-to-have-a-Serious-Talk face.

I was immediately reminded of the last time we had a Seri-ous Talk, which was over a year ago. Dad had finally discovered the reason his computer was running so slow, and instead of just going, *Oh, somebody's downloaded some rather large video files, and let me just delete them to free up some memory,* he had to go and actually *watch* them. And then he had come into my room for a Serious Talk.

"Listen," he'd said, "it's not like I didn't have a stack of *Playboys* under my bed when I was your age . . ."

"Still got 'em? They're collectors items—we could like sell 'em on eBay and probably—"

"Dec—" Yeah, to most people, "dec" is a slab of wood behind the house where you sit out and grill things and the parents get buzzed on margaritas while the kids play capture the flag in the yard. To me, it's my first name. Short for Declan. My parents were—well, Dad is, and Mom, of course, *was*, because every verb about Mom is in the past tense—big fans of Elvis Costello, who looked like a kid who gets a swirlee in the locker room. I mean, I've been dodging bullies for ten years, and I look at the guy and *I* want to give him a swirlee. And his real name is Declan. And so's mine.

"Dec," Dad had said, "I don't still have them. The point is this: it's not like I think it's some great sin to look at dirty pictures. Or, in this case, movies."

I knew it was wrong, but I just couldn't stop myself. "How'd you enjoy *The Ass and the Curious?*"

"You know—wait, is that really what it's called?"

"One of 'em, yeah."

Dad had worked very hard at that point to suppress a smile. Eventually, he won. "Anyway, it's not that that's so terrible on its own, and it's not like the death metal is so awful on its own, though I really did think you outgrew songs with Cookie Monster on vocals when you were about five"—he had given me this sly smile, like, *Hey, isn't it funny I don't understand a thing about the music you love?* I had just glared at him. "And it's not like the incredibly violent video games are so bad on their own, but put all this stuff together, and it makes me really worry about you."

"Why, Dad?"

"Because, Dec, it just doesn't . . . It's all so . . . It's all so bleak. Antiseptic phony sex scenes, guys screaming about demons eating their flesh, and hours and hours in front of the TV pretending to be a sociopathic killer. It just—geez, Dec, there's a scary amount of rage on display here."

I'd just looked at him. What could I possibly have to be enraged about? I was, at the time, a freshman boy, the lowest possible form of life in any high school. I had been desperately horny, and not into either sports or drugs, which pretty much cut out the two major avenues into the pants of eligible girls. Oh yeah, and my mom had died in a car wreck while driving me to soccer practice when I was nine. I was in the backseat and didn't get injured. I can't really say I walked away without a scratch, because they tell me the EMTs had to pull me, screaming and crying, off my mom's body. So I didn't walk. But I really didn't have a scratch.

At least Dad had never blamed me for that. Or, anyway, I never thought he did.

"So, listen, Dec," he'd said at the conclusion of last year's Serious Talk, "I've talked to your aunt Sarah, and we've agreed that you're going to spend Saturday nights over there and then go to church with her on Sunday mornings."

"Church? Church? You're kidding, right?" I had heard my dad talking to his sister Sarah after mom died and saying that any God who'd take my mom away wasn't worth getting out of bed for on Sunday.

"No, Dec, I'm not. I want . . . I feel like I'm not doing a great job—I mean, I bought you the games I'm complaining about, right? I want you to have some female influence in your life, and yeah, I do want you to go to church, even if you hate it, so it's not all demons and killing."

I had been so angry I was actually speechless, which rarely happens. "And you know, I mean, Dec, it's important for you to know that porn isn't real. I mean, they're really having sex, but that's not what real sex is like. Real sex is—"

"Dad, I swear to God I will go to Aunt Sarah's house and spend the night and go be the minister's helper if you will promise to never, ever tell me what real sex is like." I mean, who wants to hear that from their dad? *Well, son, when your mother and I used to hit it* . . . No. Not what I want to hear at all. Ever.

Dad had paused, looking like he was thinking about getting mad, and then he'd smiled. "Deal."

So that's how I came to spend weekends with my aunt Sarah, the minister at First Church, and her partner, Lisa. And how I got a job as the First Church sexton. That sounds a lot more interesting than it actually is. The sexton is actually the church janitor. So I go and sweep up the parish hall, dispose of the mouse corpses that collect in the kitchen, set some new traps, maybe rake some leaves, that kind of stuff. And the whole time, I try to figure out how I can ever say, "Yeah, they call me the sexton, 'cause I'm bringin' a ton of sex." Which doesn't even really make sense, but it amuses me when I'm doing the parts of the job that are less interesting than rodent disposal.

And I guess Dad's evil plan of a year ago kind of worked. After spending around fifty weekends at their house and three afternoons a week doing sexton stuff at the church, I now think of Sarah and Lisa a lot like real parents. I love them and they bug the shit out of me. I still listen to death metal, I still play M-rated games where I deal death and destruction, and I still look at porn.

I am now a high school sophomore, but no closer to getting to see a real girl naked, so I have to make do with digitized fantasy women, or scenarios my own fevered imagination cooks up about Neilly Foster. It sounds like a cheesy song or something, but this girl is so hot I think maybe it should be illegal. I only ever see her at lunch and in the halls—she's a junior, after all—which is good, because if I had any classes with her, I would probably fail. I once saw her eating a Popsicle in the caf and had to go home for the rest of the day.

Too bad she goes for jocks and muscleheads, which means I have exactly the same shot with her as with anybody I download on Dad's computer. There are decent girls who go for the stoners, too—bad, dangerous-looking girls, some of whom look like they might just find it interesting to introduce an innocent like myself to the mysteries of the flesh.

But here's the thing. The dildo who killed my mom was driving under the influence of alcohol, marijuana, and a couple of prescription medications. I guess it was a hell of a party.

So it's hard for me to think of the normal high school drinking and drugging as harmless party activities. I have a pretty hard time keeping my mouth shut about what weak-minded idiots people who get wasted are.

I don't get invited to a lot of parties.

But I do have some friends, though I guess they're really more school friends than home friends—the kind of people you sit next to in study hall but never call on the weekends. And I have my weekends at Sarah and Lisa's house, and I've got my metal (Did you know the coolest black metal comes from Norway? True fact!) and my games, and I choose to believe what my dad tells me—that once I get to college, girls will go crazy for a smart guy they can have a conversation with. It's hard to think about suffering through another two years of high school to get to that, but I'm comfortable enough, I guess.

Or I was, until I walk in the door—a year after our last Serious

Talk, during which time I had vainly hoped that we were through with Serious Talks forever—and I see Dad wearing that face.

"What?" I say as soon as I see him.

"Declan, we need to talk."

Oh shit. The full name. It's never good when you get off the nickname basis. I just look at him. "Well?" I say.

"Declan, I . . . I don't know how to tell you this. It's kind of a . . . I mean, I certainly never expected . . . Well, as we know all too painfully, life hands you surprises. But you know what I've found out? Not all the surprises life has in store are bad ones. Sometimes you think you have things figured out, and then, *zap!* Things change." He looks at me like he's just said something.

"Dad, what the hell are you talking about?"

"Declan, I'm getting married."

CHAPTER TWO
Neilly

HOW I ENDED UP AT A LITTLE RAINBOW-FLAG-FLYING church in the next, much cooler town over, being comforted by a guy who looks like he might just become the next big serial killer, is a pretty complicated story. For the sake of sanity—yours and mine—I've broken it down into the following heinous personal equation:

Take four stomach-acid-inducing words: *We need to talk*.

Multiply by three. (I've never believed in any superstitious stuff like *bad things come in threes* before, but after today, I just might start.)

Subtract one boyfriend and one best friend.

Add a formerly unknown, soon-to-be stepfather. (That makes

two for me in the near future—one with my mom, one with my dad.)

What does it all equal?

My life. And if you hadn't already figured this out, it's an epic mess.

The gory details: so I pretty much understood it wasn't going to be an enjoyable conversation when my boyfriend of half a year, the very sweet, very sexy, not-a-Rhodes-scholar-or-anything-but-who-cares-with-a-bod-like-that Sam uttered those words to me as I walked from AP history to media arts.

"Neilly, we need to talk."

As everyone knows, *we need to talk* is the kiss of death—to short-term plans, long-term goals, and, most especially, relationships. The second clue I was in for it: he didn't immediately shove his hand in my back pocket and pull me in close. And when he couldn't meet my eyes? Strike three, I knew for sure I was outta there.

The combo platter of what he'd said and what he hadn't done made my heart leapfrog up into my throat. "About what?" I asked, trying to keep my face as neutral as possible.

Sam stared down at his untied Pumas and took a deep breath. "I think we should see other people."

His words hit me like bullets, leaving me way more wounded than I would've expected. I mean, it's not like I was in love with the guy. And granted, he could be a total Neanderthal on the football field, as well as when he was with his boys. But over the past six months, I'd gotten to know the *real* Sam—not the big musclehead everyone at school seemed to be a little bit afraid of, but the gentle, protective teddy bear he was when it was just us two—and I'd discovered I truly liked him. A lot.

"Since when?" I felt compelled to ask once I was sure I wasn't going to croak. As far as I knew, things had been totally warm and cozy between us lately.

He shrugged, his eyes still on the floor. "This weekend, I guess."

This weekend, my dad had surprised me with a little father-daughter bonding trip to San Francisco. And in between visiting Alcatraz, Chinatown, and Ghirardelli Square, he'd been sure to point out all the happy same-sex couples. Probably so I'd know everything was going to be cool, even after he married Uncle Roger.

But the thing was, I was already fine with his lifestyle. Yeah, it had taken a while to get over the shock of his leaving my mom for a guy, and I'd definitely had to toughen up *a lot* to survive the shit I took after the kids at school found out, but really. He didn't need to fly me all the way to California to convince me he wasn't defective. I was the one who'd spent the past two years defending him, the one who was always ready to throw down anytime I heard some cretin say "That's so gay!" when really he meant something was stupid. So my dad had no worries when it came to me—I was already on board.

Sam, maybe, not as much. But even if he wasn't quite as comfortable with the whole thing as I was, he'd always stood up for me—in his own silent way, puffing out his chest and glaring at any kid who dared to bring up the subject around him. That counted for a lot in my book, and it was just another thing I was going to miss about having Sam in my life.

"Is this about my dad's commitment ceremony?" I asked gently, wondering if his mom and dad were giving him a hard time again about attending my father's wedding. "I told you, it's gonna be fine. Your parents will understand that being my date only means you're supporting me, not necessarily gay marriage."

"It's not about your dad's . . . thing. Or even my parents' opinions," he mumbled. "I just think we need some time apart, you know?"

Clearly, Sam wasn't going to explain whatever was going on here. And probably there was a whole lot more explaining to do. If I were the kind of person who didn't mind public displays of emotion, I would have definitely been bawling by now.

Good thing I am not that kind of person at all, at least not anymore.

When my parents first announced their divorce and I found out the reason why, I'd been as fragile as an eggshell. If anyone even looked at me the wrong way, I'd fall to pieces. But as time went by—and more and more kids decided the situation was funny, the stupid assholes—I'd transformed myself into the absolute queen of control. Nerves of Steely Neilly. Pinch a thigh, clench my jaw, count to one hundred backward in my head—anything so they wouldn't see me cry. I'd be damned if I was going to give anyone the satisfaction of knowing how much they'd hurt me, and Sam breaking up with me in the halls between periods three and four was no exception.

"That's cool," I finally said with a little shrug that I hoped he'd interpret as meaning I really didn't care one way or the other.

Sam dared to really look at me then, a relieved smile curving up at the ends of his lips. The ones I'd never get to kiss again. Damn. "I'm so glad you're not mad at me, Neilly. I was worried you might freak out or something when I told you."

I reached up and patted his cheek, my hands already regretting the fact they wouldn't be touching his soft-but-stubbly face anymore. "I think you know me a lot better than that."

Sam gave my shoulder an awkward squeeze and turned to walk away. He was almost halfway to the gym when he stopped short and turned back around. "Hey, Neilly?"

I was probably hoping for a movie-style ending. You know, like a touching romantic declaration—something along the lines of *I'll always remember the great times we had together. You're the only one who really understands me*—that would make the pain of the last five minutes bearable, because then I'd know the previous six months had really meant something. Instead, I got this:

"Don't listen to what anyone says. It's not you—it's me."

Though I thought I'd handled myself pretty well up until that moment, now I was *this* close to losing it. *It's not you, it's me* is such crap. It's what people say when it really *is* you but they don't have the balls to be honest about it.

I quickly put out the distress signal to my BFF. Thumbs moving furiously, I texted *3rd fl bathroom. Bldg C. Now!!!*

She hit me up immediately, just like I knew she would. *Coming.* I could always count on Lulu to have my back.

I made a beeline to the girls' room and locked myself in a stall, fingers pressing hard against my temples. I waited until I felt positive I wasn't going to cry, then flushed the toilet to make it seem like I'd been peeing the whole time, washed my hands, and splashed a little cold water on my face.

"You okay, Neilly?" I looked up to find Suzy Melendez, wannabe Gossip Girl, peering at me in the mirror like maybe if she looked long enough, she could just skip the questions and go straight to reading my mind.

I patted my face with one of those horribly scratchy brown paper towels that absorb nothing and gave her a fake smile. "Sure, fine. Just freshening up before class."

"Oh, good," she said, sounding way more disappointed than happy. "I thought maybe you were upset about what happened Saturday night."

It obviously had something to do with Sam and what he'd been up to while I was out of town with my dad. Whatever it was, I didn't want to give Suzy the satisfaction of being the one to tell me all the sordid details and then witness my sure-to-be-horrified reaction, so I bluffed my way out of it. "I know what happened this weekend," I said. "It's totally cool."

Suzy's eyes got so big and round she ended up looking like an anime character. "Wow, that's loyalty. I wish I had a friend as good as you."

I crossed my arms over my chest and leaned back against the sink—all casual, all cool, all the time. "Yup, that's me. Loyal as hell."

Before Suzy could push it any further, Lulu came flying through the girls' room door, her face all red and sweaty. I was touched she'd made such a humongous effort to get to me before the final bell, and I was just about to tell her so when Suzy started stirring things up again.

"Hey, Lulu, you're so lucky to have Neilly as a friend. I mean, she's not even mad at you for kissing Sam at Crane's party! I guess you guys really do share everything, huh?"

I blinked hard. So my best friend and my boyfriend had hooked up while I was in San Fran? I'd only been gone for two days, for chrissakes! I knew high school guys were total horndogs, but couldn't Sam have waited until I got home if he needed to make out with someone so badly?

"I wouldn't exactly say everything." I could barely see Lulu through the narrow slits that had suddenly become my eyes.

"Neilly, please. We need to talk," Lulu said, like I hadn't already figured that one out.

Suzy just stood there, probably taking notes in her head to blab and blog about later. "I thought you already heard all about this?"

"Oh, I've heard everything I need to hear," I spat, taking off with Lulu hot on my trail and Suzy stalking right behind her like the paparazzi.

"Neilly, will you please just stop and listen to what I have to say?"

Um, no, Lulu. I didn't want the entire universe to witness my complete and utter humiliation, so I picked up the pace. But just when I thought I was home free, Lu grabbed a hunk of my hoodie and stopped me dead in my tracks.

"Neilly, it's like this. Sam and I were just talking," she began, then turned to Suzy. "Do you mind? We'd like a little privacy here."

Suzy reluctantly left us alone, but I still wasn't about to let Lu get away with her lame-ass excuses. "The last I knew, talking and hooking up weren't exactly the same thing."

Lu twisted a clump of auburn hair around her finger, a habit she tends to fall back on when she's (a) nervous, (b) caught in a lie, or (c) both. I assumed it was "c" in this instance. "Please, Neilly, you have to believe me. It wasn't like that at all."

"Then what *was* it like, Lu? What could you possibly say to make this okay?"

She shrugged pathetically. "I don't know. . . . I wasn't feeling well so I was lying down . . . and then suddenly there was

Sam, telling me how much he loved you . . . and how he was worried about going to your dad's ceremony . . . and then . . ."

Her story totally wasn't working for me, so I made up a better ending. Too bad it was only make believe. "You pulled a tragic rock-star move, choked on your own puke, and he had to do mouth-to-mouth to save your life but everyone mistakenly assumed you were making out?"

Lulu opened and closed her mouth several times before any words came out. "Not exactly, but—"

"No buts, bitch. You're officially dead to me."

I stormed away as Lu yelled, "Neilly, I'm sorry! I never meant for it to happen, and it will never happen again! I'd take it all back if I could!"

It's three miles to my house from school, I am currently carless, and I was wearing fashionable but uncomfortable moccasins at the time. None of that stopped me from running like hell to get home. I just wanted to crawl under a blanket and nurse my wounded pride with Wubster (my nearly-worn-through stuffed bunny), a few episodes of *The Secret Life of the American Teenager* (my drama is nothing compared to those kids), and a pint of Cherry Garcia (my absolute favorite comfort food).

All of which was a great idea, except when I finally made it to my front door, I couldn't find my key anywhere. I patted all my pockets, checked all over the ground, searched every inch of my backpack. Still nothing. So I limped around to the backyard—blisters had replaced the things formerly known as the backs of my heels—and retrieved the spare from its hiding place inside a fake rock. (Like robbers totally wouldn't be able to tell the gray plastic thing was different than the other real brown rocks back there—but whatever, it makes my mother feel better knowing I won't ever be locked out.)

Gimping back up front, I turned the key in the lock. I wasn't expecting my mom for another five hours or so—maybe even more, since she'd been working late and traveling on business a lot more in the past few months—and I was actually grateful to be alone in my misery. My plan was to wallow a bit, rage a bit, and then make my mom feel really sorry for me when she got home so she'd totally baby me.

But a triple whammy hit me instead. I walked inside my house to find that not only was my mother already there but she was also making lunch in the kitchen wearing nothing but a towel. What's worse, a nondescript middle-aged guy, dressed in the same appalling way, was chopping vegetables right next to her. And the final kicker: he was nibbling away at the red peppers *and* my mom's ear.

"What are you doing here?" my mom finally squeaked after she was done screaming and throwing a hand over her terry-cloth-covered chest.

"I'd ask you the same thing if it wasn't so obvious." The

Secret Life marathon, ice-cream pity party, and TLC from Mommy Dearest clearly weren't meant to be.

"Neilly, we need to talk."

My mom—the one who had always prided herself on being so open with me, the one I told almost everything to and thought told everything to me—had just been revealed as a complete and utter fraud. I had no clue who the guy was, leading me to believe I didn't know who my mother was anymore, either.

"You're a grown woman. You don't have to ask my permission to get laid," I shot back at her.

My mom got that look on her face—the one where her top lip quivers right before the waterworks start. "No. But I would like your permission to get married," she said softly.

It was the final straw. After my dad announced he wanted a divorce in order to be with "Uncle" Roger—his new law partner who soon became his new life partner—my mom told me she'd sworn off men forever. I believe *all the good ones are gay* were her exact words. And now . . . this. Total shocker, and I don't mean that in a good way.

"Permission not granted!" I yelled, and slammed right back out the front door.

I quickly dialed my dad's cell, but it went directly to voice mail. I didn't even bother to leave a message, just started walking again. Eventually, I looked up and realized I had no clue what part of town I was in and no one to call to come get me anyway.

The only thing that saved me from going completely insane was the cute little church at the end of the block. It was white clapboard with an old-fashioned steeple, and it had a sign out front that read ALL ARE WELCOME, ALWAYS. I figured that must include me.

So I walked inside, looked around to see if anyone was there—it was completely empty—and plunked myself down on a worn wooden pew. And then I just sat there, staring from a stained-glass window of Jesus to the rainbow flags lining the walls to the statue of Buddha on the altar and back again, wondering what crazy kind of religion believed in all those things.

I also wondered what the hell to do next. I'd given up on church once I realized my dad wouldn't be welcome anymore in the one we used to go to. And I'd also pretty much given up on any God that would condemn a person for falling in love with someone just because they were the "wrong" gender. So I couldn't exactly sit there and pray, because if there was a God, he was probably just as pissed at me as I was at Him.

So instead, I did the only thing I could think of—I put my head in my hands and cried like a baby. All alone, with no need to pretend I didn't have feelings like I do all the time at school, my body was flooded with total relief.

Until I realized I wasn't alone at all.

"I think I know exactly how you feel right now."

For a second, I thought maybe God, Jesus, or their mutual

friend Buddha was making a private appearance. But then I saw through my tears that the voice had actually come from a scrawny, scraggly-haired guy in a black Opeth T-shirt. Though he looked like he'd never spent a single day in the sun—he was so pale I could've easily been convinced he was an honest-to-goodness vampire—and he clearly liked listening to music designed to make people want to kill themselves or each other, there was something about him that made me feel like maybe I could trust him. Which was a good thing, since I didn't have much of a choice now, did I?

"I am *not* crying," I told him, wiping away those stupid tears. "And don't you ever tell anyone I was, or I'll have to kill you."

It was such a dumb thing to say in a church, especially to a guy who looked as if he'd more likely be the one to kill me, we both started cracking up like long-lost friends.

CHAPTER THREE

DECLAN

I JUST WANT TO MAKE IT CLEAR THAT IT'S NOT LIKE I expected Dad to stay celibate for the rest of his life. I have no idea if the horniness that clouds my thinking at all times of the day and night is something that ever goes away. If not, it has probably been a really long six years for Dad since Mom died. And it's bad enough that I have to endure this torture; I certainly wouldn't wish it on anybody else.

So, yes, it has occurred to me that my weekends at Sarah and Lisa's house might serve the dual purpose of allowing Dad to discreetly get some without introducing the problem of my reaction to a new maternal figure. It was an arrangement that suited me fine. Dad has certainly been more patient and relaxed since I started spending Saturday nights away, and I do suspect this is not just because he's content that I'm getting a weekly dose of Unitarian Universalism. And I never had to meet whoever the bimbo was and have the horrifying mental picture of my dad and this woman getting sweaty together storm the fortress of my mind.

I mean, really, it was a perfect arrangement. Dad gets laid once a week, I get a more relaxed father, and I can still pretend my dad is an asexual bald guy who just happened to join a gym a year ago and has rock-hard man boobs.

But Dad had to go and ruin it. "Her name is Carmen. Carmen Foster. Her daughter, Neilly, goes to your school," Dad said, immediately after informing me that he was getting married.

It was at that point that I ran up to my room and slammed the door. I felt kind of bad about that because I was sure Dad would interpret my behavior as an indication I was so upset by his revelation that I had to stomp off and be by myself.

I did have to be by myself, but this was just because the knowledge that I would be living under the same roof as that hottie badass Neilly Foster completely shut down my brain. Neilly Foster was going to live in the same house with me. Which meant I might get to see her eat lots of Popsicles. Which meant her underwear would live here, too. Which meant she would, at least when she was in the shower, be naked in the same building as me.

The whole thing had me so excited that I was done beating off before Dad even made it up the stairs. "Dec, come on," he said, and if he hadn't been my dad, I would have said, "Yeah, I did just come on—a tissue! Ha-ha!"

In my excitement, I'd forgotten to lock the door, and Dad came walking right in. Fortunately, I had zipped up, but I still had the wadded-up tissue in my hand. It occurred to me to pretend to blow my nose in it just for cover, but I just threw it out instead.

"I can't have you running away from this conversation," Dad said. "We need to talk about this."

"I'm sorry, Dad," I said. "I was just so surprised."

"I know, and I'm sorry," Dad said. "Believe me, I never wanted to spring something like this on you."

"So why did you?"

Dad stopped and blushed and stammered. "Well, Dec, the thing is . . . I mean . . . Well . . . She's, um . . . You're going to have a little sibling."

"What? What?"

"It was just . . . It was late at night, and we'd had some wine, and we just weren't thinking, you know, we'd been very careful for months, but then we just . . . I mean, at our ages . . ."

Here's the part I still feel bad about. The whole situation was so completely absurd, so completely backasswards, with my dad shyly revealing that he'd knocked up his girlfriend because he'd ridden bareback while wasted, that I just started laughing. I mean, that was something I was supposed to spring on him, right? It was funny, right?

I mean, I was cracking up, just thinking about the birds-and-bees lecture he'd given me and the Our Whole Lives sexuality-education class he'd made me take at church, where we put condoms on bananas and learned about the responsible use of the divine gift that was our sexuality. Whenever he'd awkwardly raised the subject of sex, he'd always stressed that when I was ready, I had to make sure I was careful. And he'd gotten wasted and knocked up his girlfriend.

It was hilarious. But Dad apparently didn't think so. Which is why his eyes started filling with tears. "You know, I didn't expect you to make this easy, but you're just being cruel. We'll talk later."

He walked out and I fell on my bed laughing, knowing at the time that I should stop, that I should go apologize, that it really wasn't funny. Except that it was.

But then it got less funny almost immediately.

I put on some songs that some guy in Denmark had sent me by a German band called, I shit you not, Sins of Our Fathers.

It was interesting stuff—mostly about how they wanted to dig up their Nazi grandfathers so they could kill them again and feed their entrails to the demons they worshipped. I guess it was a little confused, but in its anti-Nazi content, it was actually remarkably positive for death metal.

As Sins of Our Fathers assaulted me with waves of gut-churning guitar hellfire, I started thinking. There were too many screwed-up parts of this to think about, but here's the one that really got me. I didn't want Dad to spend the rest of his life alone or anything, but having a kid—that was something special that he only did with Mom. Now Neilly Foster's mom was going to be, like, on an equal plane with Mom, and that wasn't right.

And it didn't take much of a psychologist to figure out what was going on here. He was starting over. I'd be out of the house in two years, and then he'd have his new little family, and he wouldn't have to look at me all the time and be reminded of the tragedy that had marred his life. He'd have a new kid and a new wife and a new life. Dad was starting over.

It got worse. Because why would he need to start over? Because he needed to have a kid he didn't hate for killing his wife.

I went to therapy. I know bad shit just happens, and it's not supposed to be my fault, but the fact is that if I hadn't forgotten my shin pads and run back into the house to get them, Mom and I would have cruised through that intersection and the drunken dildo would have killed somebody else. Or maybe there wouldn't have been a car in his way and he would have plowed into a tree and killed himself instead. And then everything would be fine.

So you can tell me that bad stuff just happens, but I know in my heart that it was my fault because it was. And every time I had cried to Dad, "I'm sorry, I'm so sorry, it's all my fault," and he'd held me in his arms and said, "No, buddy, it's not your fault, it's the other driver's fault—I never want you to hold yourself responsible for this," he'd been lying.

I guess it was good that he had told me what I needed to hear, but I really wish he'd actually believed it.

So that's how my laughter turned to tears and I started punching my bed and why I stopped talking to Dad.

He called me for dinner on Sunday night, and I ignored him. He called good night to me through my bedroom door, and I ignored him. In the morning, I sat in front of the TV and ate a bowl of Frosted Organic Lemur Flakes or whatever pseudo-healthy cereal Dad had bought while he made pancakes in the kitchen, and I got on my bike and rode to school without saying good-bye to him.

I got through lunch, but then I felt like I just had to bail on this day. It wasn't like I learned a ton on the best of days, and today I couldn't focus on anything. All I could do was sit there and think about how my dad hated me. Well, that and how I was going to work things so I could see Neilly Foster naked.

I'd like to say I'm such a sensitive lad that the only thing on my mind was my relationship with my father. But my mind kept coming back to Neilly Foster in the shower.

I guess this day was pretty much adolescence in a nutshell: I had a constant boner, and I wanted to cry.

Now, I do have enough self-control to make it through a school day without milking myself. I'm not going to be that kid who gets busted for beating off in the bathroom. That would probably land me on the sex-offender registry.

I'm also not going to be that kid who goes to cry in the

bathroom because he's afraid his daddy doesn't love him any-more. That would get me branded a hopeless wuss and raise my profile among the school's troglodyte population enough that I might as well paint a target on my head. I think that would actually be worse than being on the sex-offender registry.

But if I didn't get to either cry or beat off, or both, my head was going to explode, so I headed over to First Church to cry.

Sarah insists that the sanctuary of the church be left unlocked all the time so that those who need a quiet spot can come to pray or meditate or whatever. I guess it will continue like this until the first homeless guy decides to camp out here or some depraved teens have a drug-addled orgy among the splintery pews late one night. So far, nobody's taken advantage of it, though, believe me, I have filed this away as the most likely spot to lose my virgin-ity in the unlikely event some girl decides to notice me before College, Where Sensitive Guys Can Actually Get Some Booty. Which is how I think of it now.

Also, there's never anybody in the sanctuary actually praying or meditating. I guess there were a bunch of people in the weeks after that school bus crash two towns over, and Mom's death hit people in this church pretty hard, so Sarah set up this candle where Mom used to sit, and people came and cried around it. Or so I'm told.

Otherwise, it's always empty in here. Except today. I came in here to cry by myself, and somebody else was already in here crying. A girl.

Jesus, I wanted to shout, *you're a girl! You get to cry anywhere!*

Why do you have to hog the one spot where I can safely empty my tear ducts without getting my ass kicked?

Fortunately, I didn't shout that, because as I got closer, I thought I recognized the back of that head. I ought to—I'd spent enough hours picturing it bobbing up and down on my lap. Yep. Neilly Foster. Who apparently wasn't quite as tough as I'd always thought.

And yes, it was the Return of the Uncontrollable Boner. But something else came up, too. I knew what it was, mostly from hearing Aunt Sarah sermonize about it: compassion.

This girl was crying because she was all screwed up because her mom was marrying my dad. (And possibly because she'd have to share a house with a perverted little monster like myself. I suppose, in her position, I'd probably cry about that, too.)

I knew how she felt. In fact, I was probably the only person in town who had any idea how she felt. And she was probably the only person in town who had any idea how I felt. And if we could form a bond and get it on before our folks got married, then it wouldn't really be incest, and it might be okay, right? Nah—I knew that was almost certainly never going to happen. We lived in different worlds. Except those worlds were about to collide in my house. Or maybe hers.

"I think I know exactly how you feel," I said as I approached her pew.

She looked up, her eyes all red and puffy, her mascara smeared on her cheeks. She was completely adorable. After warning me she'd have to kill me if I told anyone I'd seen her in such a state—which was pretty arousing, but then again, Neilly Foster noticing my existence was pretty arousing—she said, "Yeah? How do you figure?"

"Well, I mean, your mom is marrying my dad, so there's that."

She looked at me like she was seeing me for the first time, which she probably was, which just seemed kind of funny considering the starring role she'd played in my fantasies for the last year or so.

"Well. Mom didn't mention you."

I couldn't help laughing. "Yeah, I seem to have that effect on women."

She gave a sad little smile, and I just wanted to keep it on her face, so I kept talking, which knowing me was probably a bad instinct. "I mean, I don't know what your exact situation is, I don't know if your dad is alive or what—"

"Alive. Marrying a man next month."

"Whoa. Probably right here in this very church. Anyway, my mom's dead, and I'm an only child, so the whole new baby thing was kind of hard to—"

"New baby? What new baby? What are you talking about?" she yelled. Her voice echoed through the sanctuary.

It occurred to me that I was the wrong person to be telling her this, and it also occurred to me that I was about to go from Strange Guy Who Comforted Me When I Was Down to Complete Freak

Who Delivered the News That Crushed My World. "Uh, well, to use my dad's words"—here I launched into my Dad impression, which I've had a lot of years to hone and which would be funny if she actually knew him—"er, um, uh, it was late, we'd been drinking, and normally we're very careful, but, uh . . . at our ages . . . well, you're going to have a little sibling."

I was afraid this would touch off another round of tears, but instead, she just started laughing. "Oh my God! My mom's knocked up!"

"I'm guessing she gave you the same 'be responsible' talk my dad gave me."

She cackled kind of hysterically, which clued me in that her laughter could turn into tears at any moment. "Only . . . oh shit . . . only every fucking time I left the house since the eighth grade! Hee-hee!"

She had a foul mouth. I didn't think I could be more smitten. Also, her laugh was infectious, and if you put aside the horrifying picture of our parents going at it and the knowledge that Dad hated me, the whole situation was pretty funny.

We sat there just laughing together for a minute. I guess we were laughing pretty loud, because the door at the back of the sanctuary opened and Aunt Sarah poked her head in.

"Dec?" she said. "Why aren't you in school?"

"I . . . I'm just so shocked by adults today and their promiscuous ways. . . ." My sentence dissolved into laughs, and Neilly, who'd been trying to pull a straight face when Aunt Sarah walked in, snorted really loud, which made us both laugh some more.

Aunt Sarah walked toward us, and I caught my breath enough to say, "Aunt Sarah . . . have you met my sister?" More snorts, more laughter, and Aunt Sarah rolled her eyes.

"I see you've gotten the news," she said, sitting in the pew in front of me.

"Oh, man, the wrong member of our family came to those OWL classes. I think Dad needed the condom-and-banana lesson."

Aunt Sarah fought back a smile and, with some effort, put on a serious grown-up face. "Okay, okay. So you needed a mental health day. And who's your friend?"

"I told you, she's my sister!"

Neilly extended her hand and said, "Neilly Foster. And I guess we are going to be siblings. Or stepsiblings. Or something. Uh, I guess I should probably go. I, uh . . . I mean, thanks for the . . . It's nice to—hey!" she said, turning to me. "I don't even know your name!"

I extended my hand. "Declan."

Neilly Foster reached out and wrapped her little hand gingerly around mine and gave it a squeeze. "Pleased to meet you, Declan."

It was all I could do to stay conscious. "You, too," I said, and watched her perfect ass as she all but ran from the church.

CHAPTER FOUR

Neilly

MY MOM.

Getting married.

With a baby on board.

Courtesy of too many glasses of wine and the unencumbered-by-a-condom sperm of the ear-nibbling towel wearer.

Was it any wonder I was running away from the news in horror? No one wants to think her mom is getting it on while she's at school and/or hanging with friends, no less getting it on and getting knocked up during those hours. It was just so . . . so . . . well, *disgusting* is a word that comes to mind. Not to mention completely nasty.

When I was little, I used to beg my mom and dad for a

sibling all the time. I think I fantasized about someone to push around in a stroller and feed bottles to, and if I'm being perfectly honest, to rule for life. But that was a million years ago.

And now—well beyond the expiration date of my desire for one—I was going to have a brand-spanking-new half brother or half sister. Not to mention a metalhead stepbrother and a severely underdressed, overly horny creeper of a stepfather.

It was just another addition to the unfathomable equation that had been my day. As a review:

4 stomach-acid-inducing words

x 3

– Sam

– his new girlfriend/my ex–best friend

+ balding half-naked guy/Declan's father/Mom's fiancé/babydaddy

+ in-utero half sibling

+ Dracula/Declan

= I'm completely screwed

And it wasn't like there was a simple solution to my problems. No *Oh, things will look different in the morning, chalk it up to a bad day and move on*. None of this was going away anytime soon.

At least Declan had been nice, making me laugh and getting me back to normal-ish. And his Aunt Sarah had been nice, too. If I hadn't felt so hysterical—giggles kept bubbling up out of my misery and turning it into a new breed of absurdist performance art—I might've even hung out a little longer in that church, making fun of our parents and their crazy situation. But I just couldn't.

So I walked outside and tried calling my dad again—and got shot directly to his voice mail again. This time, I put out a desperate SOS. "Daddy, I am having pretty much the worst day of my whole life and I could definitely use someone to talk to. Not to mention lots of cheese fries. Call me back as soon as you get this."

I pulled off the torture devices I used to call my favorite boots and started walking in the general direction of his office. I was hoping my dad would hit me right back, come pick me up, and we'd be at Meatheads digging into cheddar-covered spuds before I got even a few blocks.

Unfortunately, Dad not only didn't cut my walk short, but he was still nowhere to be found when I finally got to his place—only Uncle Roger was there. And while I liked him well enough, it's not like we're BFF or anything. He and my dad think I don't know they're living together, so the nights I spend at my dad's, Roger is noticeably absent. Plus, he's not exactly the type of gay guy women are dying to pal around with and tell all their secrets to. He's more like the Marlboro Man if he decided to switch teams—the strong, rugged, man-of-few-words type.

"Neilly!" he exclaimed when he saw me. "Shouldn't you be in school?"

I shrugged, peering around Roger's burly body to try to find my father's slight one.

"Is everything okay?" he asked.

"Not so much. Is my dad around?"

Roger slung a beefy arm around me, his super-starched shirt sleeve barely able to contain the huge bicep that hid underneath. "He's in court right now, defending a client. Should be back around five or so. Care to wait?"

I stared down at my dirty, blistered toes, scrunching them up like I do at the dentist's office to take my mind of the unpleasant proceedings. It kind of worked. "No, thanks. I should probably get going."

"You sure?" Roger asked, plunking his humongo body-builder body into an unsuspecting office chair that looked like it wanted to collapse under the pressure. "You might not know this about me yet, but I can be a pretty good listener."

I patted Roger's ginormous shoulder. He really was sweet, and I was glad my dad had found someone as loving, loyal, and protective as him. If only Sam had been like that not only when we were alone together but also when I was out of town for two tiny little days. "Roger, honestly, I just don't feel like getting into it all now. No offense."

"None taken," he said, patting the seat next to his desk. The guy was not easily dissuaded. "And anyway, you don't have to tell me *all* of it."

I considered arguing, but I was so dog tired I gave in and sat down instead. "Okay, fine. I just lost my best friend. To my very recently ex-boyfriend. And now I have no one to escort me to your commitment ceremony. Plus, my mom is knocked up and getting married, and I didn't even know she was dating anyone special."

Roger clasped his sausagelike fingers behind his head and whistled. "Doozies, Neilly. I'm sorry for your troubles."

"Me, too."

"You know, I don't think Griffin was planning on bringing a date to the ceremony. Maybe you two could go together."

I put my hands up quickly to deflect the idea—kind of like *Stop! In the name of no way!* Griffin Taylor was on my shit list for life, and I'd never even met him. Mostly because, until a few months ago, he hadn't even seen or spoken to Roger in, like, two years—he'd just shut out Roger completely when he found out his dad was gay. What a coward. I would *never* have done that to my dad, no matter how hard it had been to keep it together after the news hit the school.

Yeah, I'd heard all about how Griffin had apologized to Roger, and how Roger had welcomed Griff back into his life with open arms, and blahblahblahblahblah, but I wasn't buying any of it. Just because my dad was marrying Roger didn't mean I had to play nice with his loser son. Griffin's spiky blue mohawked head and stupid stoner eyes staring back at me from the picture on Roger's desk just sealed the deal. No way was I hanging around some drugged-out boy who so seriously lacked balls he couldn't even stand by his dad when the going got tough. Not even if it was just for one night.

"Roger, if you hadn't already noticed, Griffin and I don't exactly run with the same kind of crowd."

His eyes locked right into mine. "And like I've told you before, Neilly, Griff isn't who you think he is."

I cut Roger off before he could really get going. I know some parents can be blind to their kid's faults, but this was ridiculous. Could Roger really not see he'd spawned a hell-raising wastoid who only cared about himself? "I'm sure he is, Roger. And I'm sure he'll make some girl completely, deliriously happy. That girl's just not me."

"I meant you could go together as friends," he clarified. "Have someone to hang out with who's not over forty years old."

I shook my head, maybe a little too emphatically.

Roger patted my knee. "Fine. Just know that Griffin will be there if you decide you want to shake a leg on the dance floor or something. The band is going to be killer."

"Thanks," I said, standing up to leave. "Can you just tell my dad I stopped by?"

"Sure thing," he said. "Need a lift anywhere?"

I shook my head again. "No, thanks." I mean, where did I think I was going anyway? Not home, that was for sure. Not to Lu's. Not to Sam's. I was like a total homeless—not to mention friendless—person.

Without even really thinking about it, I soon found myself

back at the little church. Kneeling down in a pew, I clasped my hands tightly together and rested my head in them. I guess I was hoping for a miracle.

And I got one. Kind of.

"You okay?" a soft female voice asked.

I looked up to see Declan's aunt Sarah. "Not really."

Aunt Sarah slid into the pew next to me, put an arm around me, and squeezed me tight. "You've had a tough day."

I nodded. Words failed me, but Aunt Sarah didn't. She took me to her office, handed me a really bitter cup of coffee that I tried to doctor up with four packets of sugar and five little creamer cups, and let me spill my guts. What I liked most about her was that she didn't try to fix anything, like most adults do when you go to them with a problem—she just listened. Without judgment. And it was really nice to be able to let my guard down and vent freely for once.

I was still blabbing when my father finally showed up—I'd texted him where I was between the coffee-doctoring and the gut-spilling. To my surprise, he and Aunt Sarah greeted each other like total BFFs. Apparently, this was the church Dad had been trying to get me to attend with him on Sundays. While I'd been busy boycotting God, he'd gone and found a more tolerant version of Him. Here. With Aunt Sarah. Small world, huh?

So after they were done hugging and hi-ing and how-are-you-ing, my dad turned to me and said, "I'll take you home now, Neilly. Your mom has been worried sick about you."

I hadn't responded to a single one of her texts or voice mails since I'd caught her with Afternoon Delight Dude. "Dad, please. Let me stay with you, at least for a couple of days," I begged. "I don't know how I'm supposed to act normal after seeing Mom like that. I mean, I feel like I should poke my eyes out and get a lobotomy so I never have to think about it again."

"That's a little dramatic, don't you think?" he asked, putting a hand on my back and gently steering me toward the door. "Thanks, Sarah, for being such a good sounding board for my daughter today. We really appreciate it."

"And I really appreciate the difficult position she's in," Aunt Sarah said, giving me a supportive nod. "In fact, I think I just might've convinced Neilly to give my youth group a try, to help her deal with things."

"Sounds great," my dad called over his shoulder as we walked away. As soon as we were outside, he added, "I assume you were just being polite."

"I don't know. She was cool. So maybe."

My dad unlocked the doors to his old-man sedan with the automatic clicker. "Good. I really think you'd like Sarah's youth group. It's a very different kind of church than the one we used to go to, Neilly."

"So I gathered."

We drove a few blocks in silence, but just as I reached out to turn on the radio, my dad stopped me. "I know you're upset with your mom, but please give her a break. She's been through a lot."

"*She's* been through a lot?" I snorted.

"She has, and so have you," he said, turning into my driveway. "Just know she never meant to hurt you."

I shrugged. I figured it was probably true.

"And neither did I, you know?" he added.

"I know," I said, wondering why things couldn't just be easy—and normal—for a change. "I love you, Daddy."

"Love you, too, pumpkin."

CHAPTER FIVE

DECLAN

ONCE NEILLY LEFT THE CHURCH, THE WHOLE SITUATION suddenly didn't seem so funny anymore. Also, since Neilly wasn't crying (or present to witness my unmanly tears), it seemed like it was my turn. I felt my eyes fill up, and I started sniffling. Fortunately, Aunt Sarah saved the day.

"So do you want a cup of coffee or something?" Aunt Sarah asked. Sarah and Lisa are complete caffeine fiends, and they got me hooked on the stuff.

"Sure," I said. Back we went to Sarah's office, and I sat there and sipped my Equal Exchange Fair Trade Organic French Roast and sat in the comfy chair while Aunt Sarah sat behind her desk and pretended to work on her sermon. Above her head was the big banner that had hung over the church doors during the antigay-referendum thing a few years ago. LOVE MAKES A FAMILY, it read.

The coffee was bitter and dark. I take it black, like my metal.

I knew Aunt Sarah well enough to know what she was up to. Maybe this was something they taught her in minister school. Whereas Dad will pester me with questions and get a nasty argument out of the deal, Aunt Sarah's weapon is silence. She's perfectly happy to sit there all day and wait me out, figuring that I'll fill the silence.

Come to think of it, maybe introducing me to coffee was another stealth get-the-surly-teen-to-open-up move, since I get a little motormouthed when I'm under the influence.

Joke's on her—I usually talk about Norwegian black metal.

Not today, though.

Halfway through my cup of coffee, this came spilling out of my mouth: "I mean, he could have just hung up a sign that says, 'I'm done with Declan, time for act two,' right? I mean, what the hell is that about? New kid. I bet he just can't wait for me to get the hell out of the house so he can start his new, tragedy-free life with his kid who won't be damaged."

Aunt Sarah looked up from her computer. "Is that really what you think?"

"Well, it's pretty obvious, isn't it?"

She sighed, closed her laptop, and said, "Declan. You know I love you, right?"

I suddenly found my shoes very interesting. "Yeah," I said quietly. I mean, I love her, too, but it's obvious! Why make life uncomfortable by talking about it?

"So," she continued, "I want you to hear what I have to say, knowing that it comes from the deep love I have for you." I didn't say anything. "Don't be an idiot."

I've seen this in the movies but never really believed in it. But I choked on a mouthful of hot coffee and spat it on the floor of Aunt Sarah's office.

She laughed. "I was trying to get it to come out your nose, but that'll do."

I laughed in spite of myself. "What do you mean?"

"Go get a paper towel and I'll tell you."

As I wiped up the coffee, Aunt Sarah said, "Declan, your dad has been living for you for the last six years. I'm not exaggerating. I've had a lot of late-night phone calls from him when he said you were the only thing that keeps him going, that he was so grateful he had you, because if he'd lost you both in the accident, he would have killed himself."

I can feel my eyes filling up with tears again, but this time Aunt Sarah had me on the ropes and showed no mercy. "He talks about how you have these facial expressions like your mom had, and how you are the only part of her he has left."

Oh, that was below the belt. "So now he's getting rid of both of us," I managed to sniff out before a really embarrassing sob escaped. Aunt Sarah waited until I got myself under control.

"He's not getting rid of you, Declan. He's giving you a new life."

"Well, I liked the old one."

"Yeah, that's why you immerse yourself in music and games that are all about death."

Call me an idiot, fine. But don't mess with my metal. We've had this discussion before. Like, don't you think it's a little sick the way that most of the culture denies death? It's there all the time, and most people act like it's not going to happen to them. I guess it would be better if I listened to some bullshit pop music about girls with big asses dancing.

"Hey, great pastoral counseling there, Reverend. I feel tons better. Thanks." I walked out of her office and headed home.

When I got home, I cranked up some Norwegian metal, popped Hitman 2 into the Xbox, and spent a nice long time "immersing myself in death."

But here's why Sarah is an idiot about this stuff—I felt so much better after a couple hours of this. Like I could look Dad in the eye when he came home and actually apologize for being an asshole to him. I mean, I was still pissed, but he is giving me a chance to be in the same building as a naked Neilly Foster, and I do appreciate that. And I didn't know that stuff about him living for me or whatever. Basically, I have no idea how to feel, but at least having had my ass kicked by some growling Norwegians helped me to feel the bad stuff strongly enough that I could put it away for a while. Or maybe not. I have no idea.

The rest of the week was pretty normal. I guess maybe I spent even more time than usual listening to metal and playing video games, but every time I turned around, Dad was there trying to have some kind of meaningful conversation, and I just had to duck out of those. I mean, I figure if we can coexist peacefully in the house, let's do that—why mess with success by talking stuff over?

I saw Neilly in the halls three times over the course of the next week. Every time she saw me she at least nodded her head in my direction, and I give her a lot of credit for that. Because, let's face it, she's got everything to lose and nothing to gain by being nice to me in the Darwinian jungle of high school. Well, I mean, okay, it's not like she stopped and had a conversation with me, but at least she acknowledged me as a fellow human being, which most of the kids who occupy the top of the social totem pole at our school would never do.

Well, there are the two football players who think it's really hilarious to call me "Columbine" every time they see me. I'm not sure if that counts. I suspect it doesn't.

Of course, even if Neilly had stopped to talk to me, I probably wouldn't have been able to talk to her, because a great deal of my mental energy was now devoted to the forbidden-love-between-stepsiblings fantasy.

I'm lying. It was much more of a forbidden-sex-between-stepsiblings fantasy. It's not like I wanted to sit in the stands at the football game holding hands with her or take her to the stupid prom or whatever.

This is why, that weekend, I was tongue-tied when she showed up after church as I was vacuuming the parish hall. Well, that and the fact that she was in the backseat of my dad's car with her mom in the front seat. Well, plus the fact that my Dad had just unexpectedly picked me up at church and said, "It's open house day, and we're going to go look at houses!"

I stood there for a minute. I guess I was dumbstruck. I guess maybe the caffeine I'd just pounded at coffee hour hadn't kicked in yet. Finally I came up with, "Um, why?"

"Well, Carmen's house is too small, unless you and Neilly want to share a bedroom, ha-ha"—oh, please God, make it financially impossible for us to do anything but move into Carmen's house— "and our house . . . well, you know."

"I'm afraid you're gonna have to help me out on this one, Dad."

"I just couldn't . . . I couldn't share the same room with Carmen that I shared with your mom. I just couldn't do it."

See, now they try to convince me that this isn't about Dad trying to put my mom and me behind him, and then he tells me he's selling the fucking house. So he won't ever have to look at the place where I was a kid again.

"You know . . . do you think you could just tell me something in advance once in a while? I'm getting pretty sick of you surprising me with stuff. You got any other plans to turn my life upside down? Because I think I'd like to know in advance for once."

Dad got frustrated. Good. "Dec, you know what? Ugh, just get in the car. We'll talk later."

"Like hell." I stormed over to the car and found my seat occupied by Carmen Foster and the backseat occupied by Neilly Foster. I was still really pissed off. But on the bright side, I was going to the backseat of my dad's car with Neilly Foster. There were literally hundreds of guys in school who would probably kill to be able to say they went to the backseat of their old man's car with Neilly Foster. And if you took a vote among the student body for Most Likely to Go to the Backseat of Their Old Man's Car with Neilly Foster, you would not find me in the top five hundred.

I climbed into the backseat and saw Neilly sulking. "Hey," I said.

"Hey," she said.

"Did you know about this?"

"*No!*" Neilly said to her mom.

Her mom ignored her and turned around and said, "Declan? It's great to meet you. I'm Carmen." She extended a hand, which I didn't want to shake, but I didn't want to piss off Neilly by being a dick to her mom, so I said "Hi" and shook her hand.

And yeah, she was a total MILF, but the implications of that were just so weird that I quickly turned the full force of my perverted imagination on Neilly, who was wearing shorts.

We studied Greek mythology in the ninth grade, mostly so we could read *The Odyssey*, which I actually kind of liked because there was sex and gore in it. One thing I remember was that in the Greek hell there was this guy who was standing in a pool of water with a fruit tree hanging over his head. Every time he reached up for the fruit, the tree would shoot just out of his reach, and every time he reached down to get a drink, the pool would dry up. I can't remember what he did to get to hell, but it must have been pretty bad for him to be punished by being so close to the things he wanted so badly and never being able to touch them. This is pretty much what it was like for me to be in the backseat of a car with Neilly Foster's bare thighs.

We rode in silence to some house, and Dad and Carmen got out and circled to the side of the car, while Neilly and I sat motionless. I guess Neilly was still sulking. As for me, I had shorts on and a boner, so I figured I'd just hang out in the backseat until I could get my mind onto something unsexy. I thought about asking Dad to help a brother out by flashing some back hair, but I didn't think he'd think that was funny in front of his girlfriend, fiancée, baby-mama, whatever the hell this woman was.

"Are you guys coming?" Carmen asked in a fake-perky way.

"*No!*" Neilly yelled again.

"Dec?" Dad said.

"Tell you what. How about you guys just pick out a house and buy it and tell us the day before we have to move. Okay?"

Dad looked mad. Carmen came around the car and linked her

arm into his and said, "Okay, guys, we're gonna go poke around. And I promise you we won't buy anything without your approval. We thought this would be kind of fun for you guys, but I guess we made a mistake. I'm sorry."

They walked into the house, leaving Neilly and me in the backseat. I had to speak lest my brain explode. "Well, this is a pisser."

"Tell me about it. I mean, I'm not that sorry to leave our house. I'm just tired of her making these decisions about my life without saying anything to me."

"Yeah. This whole thing sucks."

"Is your house nice? You like it, I mean?"

"I don't know. It's a house. It's just that . . . Well, forget it."

"What?"

"I just remember my mom there."

She didn't say anything for a minute, and I sat there getting angrier and sadder, and finally I felt like I really needed to kick something, like my skin was tingling and the only way to release that energy was to commit some kind of physical violence. Seeing me spazzing out and hitting stuff was not the kind of intimacy I craved with Neilly Foster, so I just said, "I gotta bail. I'll see you later," and got out of the car.

I didn't even know where the hell I was; I only knew that I wanted to be somewhere else. I started just walking down the street, figuring I'd eventually come to something I recognized. It wasn't like it was that big of a town.

I got about a block away when I heard something behind me. I was glad Dad had come running after me. I turned around to tell him we couldn't leave Mom behind, that I knew it was dumb, but that I felt like she'd still be in that house and we'd be living somewhere else and she'd be gone forever.

What I saw instead of Dad was Neilly Foster bouncing toward me. "Hey!" she called.

"Yeah?"

"You can't just leave me alone with them! How would you like it if you had to spend the day with just them?"

I stopped. "Um, I don't know. I guess that would suck."

"Goddamn right it would. I sent Mom a text message and told her we'd be at our house. Come on."

"You live around here?"

"Like, three blocks away."

We walked to Neilly's house, and I was still so upset thinking about Mom that I forgot to be lustful. I felt like I was on the verge of tears the whole time, and I was really afraid I was going to cry in front of her, so as soon as we got in the door, I said I needed the bathroom and ran in. Of course, once I was alone, I didn't need to cry anymore. What the hell was up with that?

I looked around. A bathroom in a house shared by two women is just not the same type of room as a bathroom in a house shared by two men. For one thing, there was this little thing on the back of the toilet—it looked like a collection of metallic ivy. One tissue poked out of the top. I guess the rest of them were in there somewhere, disguised under the artsy ivy. Why the hell would you want to pretend your snot rags were growing out of the woods? There was a bowl of some dried flowers and bark and stuff—it smelled pretty good. Next to the sink there were these little round soaps that looked like they'd never been used. Hanging next to the sink were three towels that were the exact same shade of yellow that covered the walls. They also looked like they'd never been used. I wondered if women's dirty little secret is that they don't wash their hands just so they can keep their bathrooms looking nice. Dad cleans the bathroom regularly at our house, so it's not like some gross gas station bathroom or anything, but we don't have any tissues on the back of the can, we don't have any bowls of bark, and we only have one slimy bar of Ivory that we both use to wash our hands. I can't even imagine wanting to spend any energy at all making the place where you shit look pretty. Clean, I get. Pretty—no. And yet, this was how it was going to be—no more old *New Yorker*s next to the toilet, no more rectangular soap, no more plain white towels.

I splashed some water on my face, flushed the toilet, and left the bathroom. I found Neilly in the kitchen eating ice cream. "Want some Karamel Sutra?" she asked.

I briefly choked on my own spit. "Some what?"

"Karamel Sutra! It's my favorite flavor."

"Yeah. Yes, I do."

"I got you a bowl and a spoon. They're over there next to the sink." The sink was not piled up with dishes from breakfast or from last night's dinner. Another way I knew I wasn't in my own house.

I scooped myself some ice cream and sat down at the table.

"I wonder," Neilly said.

Whether dorks are good in the sack? Try me, baby—unpopular guys work harder! "What?"

"Whether it would be possible to, you know, break them up or something."

"Sounds kinda *Parent Trap*."

"Yeah, only in reverse."

"Well, listen, if you can somehow get Lindsay Lohan involved, I'm in. Otherwise, I don't think it's such a great idea."

"Ew, she's like ten in that movie!"

"Yeah, but she's not ten now, is she?"

"No, but she's kind of a skank."

"Exactly. Anyway, I did think about this. I mean, this may come as a surprise, but I can be a total dick if I want to be. I'm pretty sure I could send your mom screaming for the exits if I put my mind to it."

She took a minute and looked at me. "You know, no offense, but I think maybe you could."

"None taken. I pride myself on my ability to offend. But anyway, I don't want to do that."

"Why not?"

"Because—I don't know how long ago your parents split, but my mom's been dead for six years. And growing up without one of your parents totally sucks, and I don't want that for my little brother."

She smiled. "You mean my little sister."

"Whatever." I ate some more ice cream.

"You think we could all fit in your house?"

"Well, I suppose Junior's gonna need his own room at some point. I mean, I would not really want to share. I'm not hip to the whole two a.m. feeding thing, and, you know, I can't have my baby brother crampin' my style when I have a lady over."

Neilly looked at me skeptically but was nice enough not to interrogate me on exactly which ladies had ever set foot in my room. None, of course, but I wanted to have the option, which I certainly wouldn't have if Junior was shitting his diapers in a crib in the corner. Though I suppose that might allow me to be able to say, *Hey, baby, wanna come back to my crib?* with a straight face.

"Well, this place is definitely too small for a fam—for five people," Neilly said. She ate her ice cream in silence for a while, so I did the same. I was glad she'd stopped herself. A family was Mom and Dad and me. Dad and I might live in the same house as Neilly and Carmen, but that wouldn't make us a family.

The silence started to feel awkward. I didn't know what to say—can I see your room? Can I have a few minutes alone with your underwear drawer? And then I remembered something from this morning.

"Hey, I have a question."

"Yeah?"

"Is your dad . . . is he like a big guy with a mustache? Looks like he does ultimate fighting in the hot sun all day?"

She snickered. "Not hardly. That sounds like my uncle Roger. He's my dad's . . . well, you know, the person he's committing to, or whatever. Why do you ask?"

"He stood up in church today and said this long thing about how much it meant to him that there was a church that would recognize and celebrate who he really was, stuff like that." Neilly looked pained. "I'm sorry. Is that like a sensitive subject or something?"

"Only the fact that I got dumped and have to show up alone for their ceremony, like a loser," she said.

My brain was reeling. Neilly Foster got dumped? It boggled my mind. What must it be like to be the guy who gets so much play he can confidently show one of the hottest girls in school the door? I didn't know whether I wanted to kill the guy or beg him to teach me his secrets. Maybe both. But not in that order. "Yeah," I said, "I remember the pain of being dateless. Pretty horrible."

She raised an eyebrow at me again. "Do you have, like, some harem of metal babes or something?"

No, because it's pretty tough to find a metal chick who doesn't drink or get high. "Oh, hell yeah. Tattoos, piercings, the whole thing. You know, you haven't lived until you've felt a pierced—"

"Okay, okay. Enough. Well, lucky you. As for me, I got on the wrong train. I was pretty sure I wasn't headed to Loserville, but I guess life hands you surprises."

"Yeah." Incredible—how could anybody in Neilly Foster's position be unhappy? I mean, being unhappy about your mom being knocked up by my dad, and having to move, and gaining a weird stepsibling: I get all that stuff. But, I mean, Jesus. She could walk into the hall and whisper, "I need a date," and probably have a hundred guys lined up within thirty seconds. And she was putting up with a guy making her miserable.

I had a terrible epiphany at that moment. I had thought I didn't understand girls because I never got near them, but here I was, sitting in Neilly Foster's kitchen eating ice cream with her, and I had no fucking idea what made her mind work. So it wasn't proximity that was the problem. It was that they are fundamentally unknowable. Great. I was convinced if I could just figure out how girls thought, I could somehow overcome my lack of athletic ability and my dislike of booze—not to mention my skinny frame and corpselike pallor—and somehow hoodwink a girl into bed with me. But now it was clear that nobody with a penis could ever figure out how girls thought. And I had no Plan B.

"Well, have you asked his friends?" I asked.

"What are you talking about?"

"Your ex. Jocky McMoron, whoever the hell he was."

"His name is . . . Yeah, okay, Jocky McMoron is close enough. You think I should ask his friends out?"

"Yeah, why not?"

"Why?"

This gave me a ray of hope—she clearly had no idea how guys' minds worked, either.

"Well, he dumped you, but that doesn't mean he wants his friends dating you. He wants you sitting at home all by yourself being miserable, so if he gets bored of whatever ho he's with now . . ."

"That would be my *ex*–best friend."

"Hoey McMansstealer?"

She laughed. "The very same."

"Okay, so he wants you at home crying over him so when he decides he's bored of Hoey, he can scoop you up again. You're the backup plan. Every guy always has a backup plan." True—I even had a backup doomed crush. This brainiac girl named Chantelle. Her glasses said "studious," but her body said "sinful."

"And what's the best way to show him that you're not at home waiting for him? By scooping up his best bud."

She thought about it. "That's truly evil. I kind of like it."

"Evil is my specialty. But don't worry. I promise not to be evil at your dad's ceremony."

"What are you talking about?"

"Well, any time there's a big function at the church, that's extra work for the sexton."

"What the hell's a sexton?"

"It's me. I clean the church, mow the lawn, stuff like that."

"Why are you called a sexton?"

Oh, I had been waiting so long for this moment. "'Cause I'm bringin' a ton of sex," I said, grinning.

Neilly cracked up. "That doesn't even make sense! You could have said ''cause I get a ton of sex,' and that would have at least been coherent, even if it is a lie."

"Hey, I—"

"I know, I know, the piercings. Spare me," she said.

We both laughed, and just then something horrible happened. Dad and Carmen came in and saw Neilly and me eating ice cream and laughing together, and they both got all misty-eyed, and I really wanted either to vomit or to sulk again, but I couldn't because I felt better.

CHAPTER SIX
Neilly

"SO, IS IT ALL STARTING TO SINK IN?" MY MOM ASKED as she plopped herself down on my bed.

I looked up from my chem homework. "Which part?"

She smoothed her loose T-shirt over her growing belly bump. "My being pregnant, for starters."

I shrugged. "Probably not that, or really any of it, to tell you the truth."

My mom absentmindedly picked up Wubster and hugged him to her. I had to resist the urge to snatch him back. "Well then, is there anything I can do to make things easier on you?"

"Short of rewinding the past month or so, no."

My mom deposited Wubster back on my bed, stood up, and

stuck her hands on her hips. "I know you're a teenager and that entitles you to be self-centered, but this is ridiculous. Can't you think of someone besides yourself for once?"

I stared up at her with my mouth hanging open. "What?"

I mean, I wasn't only thinking about myself. I was also thinking about Lulu. And Sam. And Dec. And Dec's dad. And how two people I'd invited into my life suddenly weren't in it anymore, and how two people I hadn't invited in suddenly were.

"You heard me, Neilly Foster. It's taken me a long time to find happiness. I thought I could never trust a man again, but then along came Thomas, and I'm like a schoolgirl. Head over heels in love. I get to start over, Neilly. Do it right this time. Don't diminish that for me with your sulking."

Her eyes were boring a hole into mine, I guess looking for me to approve of her completely turning our lives upside down. Or at the very least, to forgive her for suddenly sticking me with an entirely new "family" and deciding we'd all be moving into the freakiest crib in town together as quickly as possible. Yeah, not so fast, bucko.

As if the whole living-with-a-bunch-of-strangers thing wasn't bad enough, the actual house we'd be living in was straight out of a horror movie—an ancient Victorian creepfest with peeling paint, uneven angles, a weird portico, and even a few turrets thrown in for kicks. Inside, it smelled like a combo platter of mold and old people. I was worried my new little sister—I figured this baby had to be a girl, so I could teach her how not to get burned by her BFF and BF when her back was turned— would be a nervous wreck living there.

Even as a fetus.

In fact, she was probably curled up inside my mom right this very moment, hands at either side of her face, looking like a baby version of that famous Edvard Munch painting, *The Scream*. Either that or the kid from *Home Alone* when he finds out his parents left him behind.

"Mom," I sighed, "I am happy for you. I'm just unhappy for me, you know what I mean?"

Her eyes welled up, and one salty tear made its way down her cheek. "See? That's just the kind of thing I don't need to hear!"

"You asked," I told her. "And if you didn't want to know how I felt about it, maybe next time you should consider the fact that I might not answer exactly the way you'd like."

My mom finally lost it and huffed out of the room. "You are infuriating, Neilly Foster," she called over her shoulder as she left. "It's like you're thirteen all over again. No, wait—it's like I don't even know you anymore!"

What my mom didn't seem to realize was I felt the exact same way about her. Ditto for Sam and Lulu. And out of all of them, Lulu was, in my opinion, the only one even trying to fix things.

When I'd flat-out refused to speak to her, she'd tried every electronic avenue possible to apologize for scamming Sam while I was away. And more than once, I'd almost let her slide. But realistically, how could I? If I did, wouldn't it send the wrong message? Like *Sure, go ahead, girls, make out with my boyfriend when I'm not there. It's okay, I'm a total doormat! I'll still be your friend!*

Nope, I was stuck between a rock and a hard place. Forgive Lulu and look like a complete wuss. Don't forgive her, and be so fucking lonely it physically hurt sometimes. I chose fucking lonely and left it at that.

Really, the only thing that had been worse than losing my best friend was losing her at a time when I so desperately needed her advice. Like, for instance, what in the hell was I supposed to do about being dateless for my dad's wedding? In my mind, going stag would make it seem like I was ashamed of Roger and him—like I was as bad as Roger's son Griffin—and I most certainly was not.

So who could I get to take me?

When we were house hunting with our parents—very reluctantly, I might add—Dec had suggested I ask one of Sam's friends. I think his exact words were: *And what's the best way to show him that you're not at home waiting for him? By scooping up his best bud.*

The problem here was, I didn't particularly *like* any of the guys Sam ran with—they were all kind of grunty and caveman-y.

Still, I'd tried to put the piece of advice to good use. At a party this past weekend, I'd cornered Tanner McManus while he was filling up at the keg.

"Hey, Tanner."

"Hey, Neilly," he said, tipping his cup against the tap so he'd get the maximum amount of beer and minimum amount of foam. "What's up?"

"This party sucks. Feel like going for a walk?"

He took a big slug of his drink. "Love to," he said. And then he kind of leered at me with this little foam mustache on his upper lip. He looked like a poster boy for a "got beer?" campaign. There was no way I was going to kiss the big doof now. No way I was going to kiss him *or* ask him to take me to the wedding. No way, no how.

"Cool," I said. "I'll meet you out back in a minute. I just have to fill up, too." I held up my half-full water bottle like I intended to put beer in it. Tanner didn't seem suspicious at all. Probably because he's not that smart when he's sober, but his IQ falls to somewhere around that of a doorstop when he's drunk.

"I'll be waiting," he said, slurring a little bit. Then he lumbered off, foamy lip and all.

I snuck out the front door and never looked back.

On Monday, Tanner told anyone who would listen that I wanted him, adding, "And I woulda nailed her, too, but I didn't want to be uncool to Sam 'cause he and Neilly just broke up," making it seem like *he'd* rejected *me*.

Clearly, it was time for Plan B—the ceremony was only a month away—though I had no idea what that might be. And so I decided to try Aunt Sarah's youth group. I figured it had to be better than going to a lame-ass party and trying to convince myself to hook up with Tanner McManus, and maybe it'd even give me some new ideas about how to fix my life.

When I went to tell my mom I was going, she was sitting at the kitchen table with a steaming mug in front of her. She was staring into it like she could read the future in her tea leaves or something.

"Life doesn't always go in the direction you think it should, you know," she said without even looking up. "The key is to just hang on and enjoy the ride."

"Right, Mom," I said, wondering how she expected me to enjoy a ride that took barf-inducing turns every other second. "Okay, well, I'm heading out now for that youth group at Dec's aunt's church."

My mom eyed me suspiciously. "That what?"

It wasn't exactly something I'd ever expressed an interest in before. "Um, I'm going to the youth group at Declan's aunt's church? You know, the same one where Dad and Roger are getting married?"

That's when mom broke out into this humongous smile.

"You're going with Dec? I am so glad you two are becoming friends!"

Not exactly, I thought. Under any other circumstances, we'd probably never have met, never have spoken a word to each other. So maybe *friends* was a little too strong of a word—but we were definitely allies by this point. "So I'll see you later, okay?"

"Of course," she practically trilled, happy again. Oh, the joys of impending motherhood and the roller coaster of emotions it apparently brought along with it. I made a mental note to wait until I was dead to try that one.

Half an hour later, I was sitting cross-legged on the floor of the little old church's basement. I had barely registered anything Aunt Sarah was saying, due to the fact that I was too busy drooling over the mesmerizingly hothothottie leaning against the wall by the door. He looked just like Travis from We the Kings.

"Earth to Neilly," Dec said, jabbing me in the ribs with his elbow.

I'd been so busy ogling, I hadn't even noticed he was in the same room as me. "Huh?"

"It's nice to acknowledge a soon-to-be family member when he's sitting right next to you."

"Sorry," I whispered, trying not to let Aunt Sarah know I was chatting—not to mention ogling—when I should have been thinking pious thoughts and listening. "Are you late because you had to finish up with one of your heavily pierced chicks?"

"Had to finish up my sexton duties," he whispered back.

"Because you bring a ton of sex, right?"

"A *ton* of sex," he agreed, and we both tried not to crack up. It didn't work very well. Aunt Sarah gave us a look, but her mouth was turned up just a bit at the sides and her eyes were warm and crinkly, so I knew she wasn't really mad.

"Tonight we're going to have some fun with our senses," she said, passing around a box of silky black blindfolds. "Turning some off, and turning some on."

"Kinky," Dec whispered to me.

"This is going to be way more interesting than I expected," I whispered back.

"Now everyone stand up and cover your eyes," Aunt Sarah said. "No peeking. I'm going to pair you guys up, and the first thing I want you to do is find something you have in common. Just one little thing. The only rule here is, no exchanging names or where you go to school. It's too easy to prejudge someone that way."

Soon I felt Aunt Sarah's hand on my back, and I shuffled across the room in pure blackness. "There you go," she said, placing my hand in one much larger than my own. It fit perfectly, like mine used to fit in Sam's. At this point, I actually started silently chanting *Please let it be him* in my head. Meaning the Travis look-alike.

"Hey," I said.

"Hey yourself."

His fingers gripped mine gently, sending little electrical currents shooting across my palms. "So, what do you think? Should we play along or just hang out?" I asked.

"I say we be overachievers and find something big we have in common instead of just something little."

"Okay," I said, my brain going in total slow motion. Tumbleweeds practically blew through my gray matter as words continued to elude me.

After a while, the guy helped me out with a little prompt. "Sooooo . . . how about you tell me something you believe with all your heart?"

I considered making a joke about the tooth fairy or Santa, but rejected them as too obvious. Not to mention sarcastic, and sarcasm is something I tend to rely on too heavily as it is. After a little more thought, it dawned on me that what I really wanted to say was *Love will find a way*, but I was choking on how cheesy and chick-y it would sound.

So in the end, I went with, "I guess I believe everything happens for a reason, though I don't really know why I'm saying that, because my life kind of sucks right now. And what's the reason for that?"

I was appalled at myself for spewing the unplanned verbal

vomit. But the guy—whoever he was—didn't seem fazed in the least bit. "I think 'everything happens for a reason' is probably something we tell ourselves because we'll never really know what the reasons are."

"You think?"

"Yeah. Like, what possible good reason could there be for little kids getting cancer or thousands of people dying after some lunatic crashes a plane into their office building? And where's the good reason for so many people in third-world countries living in poverty while we sit here on our fat asses wasting water and food and our lives?"

I was impressed by how deeply the guy seemed to feel—and how seriously he seemed to take—everything. "Okay, now that we've established what you don't believe in—that everything happens for a reason. Maybe you could tell me what you *do* believe with all your heart."

He paused, then said, "I guess that love will find a way."

"Me, too," I whispered, my heart beating so loud I was positive he could hear it.

I was pretty interested in finding out what else I had in common with this guy, but then Aunt Sarah announced we should all stop talking. Though there had been quite a bit of buzzing conversation and laughter before, now silence broke in. Eventually, she took me by the hand and led me back to my original place on the carpet.

"You can take off your blindfolds now," she announced.

A second later, we were all blinking and staring around the room, looking a little disheveled and a lot confused. And the hot guy was nowhere to be found. I was way more disappointed by this fact than I had any right to be.

"So can any of you tell who you've been talking to just by looking around this room?" Aunt Sarah asked.

For me, at least, the answer to Aunt Sarah's question was no. I had no clue who I'd just had such an intimate conversation with—just a supreme hope that it was my disappearing Travis look-alike. Almost everyone shook their heads along with me.

"And did any of you feel close to the person you were paired with, even though you couldn't see them?"

Nods yes, all around. Especially for me.

"I want you to remember that feeling the next time you're praying, whether that's to God or Jesus or Mother Earth or whomever. Just because you can't physically see the presence of love and goodness doesn't mean it doesn't exist. Everything you need is out there in the universe—but it's up to you to believe in it, to find it, and to let it in. Even if it's from an unlikely source," she told us. "Next session, we'll probe further into this little mystery. Until then, be good—and be open to all the goodness in the world!"

Kids started piling out the door, all wondering out loud who their partner might have been. I grabbed Dec. "I think I'm in lust."

"Well, hallelujah," he said. "I've been waiting all year to hear you say that!"

I punched him in the arm. "Goofball."

He pretended to wipe away a fake tear. "You mean, not with me?"

I gave him a look.

"So I'm guessing the lust is for the guy Aunt Sarah paired you with then?"

"Well, maybe," I said, "*if* he was the hottie standing against the wall at the beginning of group. He totally disappeared after the game—poof! like magic—before I could find out whether he was my partner or not."

"I think that was Criss Angel on the flat screen in the rec room, Colonel Mustard."

"It was not," I protested. "He was real."

"Whatever you say."

"Well, what about you?" I asked. "Did you wow all the chicks by telling them you wielded a big broom or something?"

"Nah," he said. "The only girl I talked to other than you was my partner for the cheesy get-to-know-you game. And then I was feeling more subtle, what with the blindfold."

"Was she metal enough for a guy like you?"

"Nope," he said, "but she's still sizzling."

I gave him a squinty-eyed, suspicious look. "How would you know?"

"Because I peeked."

"You sneaky bastard!" I said, impressed that Dec had blown off all the rules of his aunt's church game. "You wouldn't have possibly peeked at my guy while you were at it . . . ?"

Dec shrugged. "I might've caught a tiny glimpse."

"*Please* tell me he looked like Travis from We the Kings," I begged.

"He just looked like a regular guy. Not like any rock star I've ever seen."

I scuffed my black Converse against the cement floor. "Bummer."

I knew the love-at-first-sight—and then without-sight—theory I'd been conjuring up in my head was too good to be true. Because if my blindfolded partner was, say, Mr. Forever 21 Purple Skinny Jeans, we just weren't going to click on a physical level.

And knowing my luck, the hottie probably wasn't my partner at all—but he probably was just another dickhead.

CHAPTER SEVEN

DECLAN

DAD IS SUCH AN ASSHOLE. I MEAN, I HAD A REALLY great sulk going on that I figured I could keep going more or less until I graduated. I was prepared to stay mad at him, at least on a low level, for many hundreds of days.

And then he had to go and do something really cool. He and his babymama went and bought the single coolest house in our bullshit cookie-cutter suburb. I mean, this thing looked like the Addams Family moved out of it because it was *too* creepy. It was awesome.

It was also a total wreck. Which I thought was cool—it was more metal that way. I could totally picture Demonic Stain, my new favorite Scandinavian metal band, shooting a video in the entrance hall. When Dad heard me gurgling under my breath about Satan rending my flesh as we walked through, he just smiled and said, "I take it that means you like it?"

"Dad," I said, "this is the most metal place I have ever even thought of. It's the most metal place anybody's ever thought of."

"Well, Jimmy Page did buy Aleister Crowley's house," Dad said, smiling. "I looked into that, but, you know, it turns out to be in another country."

I cracked up at my dad, the least cool person on Earth, invoking Aleister Crowley, famous English occultist. "Do what thou wilt," I growled at Dad, because lots of metal bands used that Crowley quote.

"You know, they always get that quote wrong," Dad said.

"What do you mean?"

"I mean, what he actually said was: 'Do what thou wilt. This shall be the whole of the law. . . . Love is the law, love under will.' Now, I don't really understand what he's getting at there, but it's a little more complicated than just do whatever you feel like. I think he's working with a different definition of will than the one we use today."

I was literally speechless. "Who the hell are you, and where's my dad?"

"Dude," Dad said in this stoner drawl, "if it has anything to do with Led Zep, I know it."

Led Zep. I mean, I guess it shouldn't be surprising that my dad is into some geezer band they play on Cadillac commercials, but it was. I mean, as long as I can remember, Dad's musical taste has run to Whatever Crap They're Currently Selling at Starbucks.

So Dad was suddenly acting cool and buying the Mansion of Metal. But then he told me he was going to fix it up, which, I mean, I have to say I understood. I didn't want my baby brother killing himself on some splintery door frame or getting a shock from the exposed wiring or taking a rusty nail through the foot.

And then he did something else cool. He wanted me to help him fix it up. For money. So I could supplement my sexton salary with some carpentry cash and learn some cool stuff in the process. In the unlikely event that I ever got a date, I might actually have some cash to spend on taking the girl someplace.

They closed on the house in record time—a quick computer search showed it had been on the market for a full five years, so we were in there painting and hammering within two weeks.

"Trust me," Dad said one day as we were retiling the bathroom, "when you get to be an adult, the ability to do stuff like this will be way more attractive to a woman than the ability to catch a stupid ball."

I looked at him—what little hair he had on his head was full of dust, his clothes were filthy, and his lush carpet of back hair was poking out of the back of his T-shirt collar—and I figured, well, if this guy can bag a MILF like Carmen Foster, maybe there's something to what he's saying.

"Yeah, I'd like to not have to wait till I'm forty to have a girl-friend, thanks," I said, and then I nearly clapped my hand over my mouth. That one sentence was more information than I'd given Dad about my inner life in the last three years. He kind of beamed at me, which made it much worse.

"You won't have to wait that long," he said.

"Yeah, right. 'Hey, baby. Want me to retile your bathroom?' Not exactly a great pickup line."

Dad laughed. "It is if you use the phrase 'lay some tile.'"

It was at this point that I actually hooted with laughter. I don't know if it was the manly act of sweating together, but my dad was suddenly approximating somebody cool. And we were spending all kinds of time together and having fun and stuff, which made it a lot harder for me to believe that the whole Carmen thing was about him wanting to get rid of me.

Ah, Carmen. I knew there was something I could stay mad at Dad about. He was happier and cooler than I could ever remember him being, but we were still packing up our house, the place where I could actually remember Mom being, the place where some part of me was convinced her ghost would be hanging around the house looking for us after we left.

Not that Dad didn't try to outflank me on that score, too. I was in my room with Demonic Stain cranked up on my headphones, when the last track, "Blood of the Demiurge," finished, and my ears took in silence for a few seconds.

And I heard something weird. It sounded like this: "Hoo-hoo! Hoo-hoo!" All I could think was that Dad also had headphones on and was singing along to "Sympathy for the Devil," which is one of the only geezer rock songs I can stand. I thought the sight of my dad rockin' out Mick Jagger–style might be pretty funny, so I snuck over to his room to have a look.

I took my camera.

And then I had to kind of hide my camera behind my back, because Dad was there on the floor of his room, not singing along with Mick at all, but crying. And not some manly, tears-trickling-down-the-cheeks crying, but full-on girly sobbing, complete with the aforementioned "Hoo-hoo!" I was embarrassed for him and for me, and I was getting ready to bail when he looked up at me. He was on the floor in front of Mom's closet, and he was putting stuff into a box. Not important stuff like her ashes or anything, just stupid stuff that he'd never gotten rid of—the shoes she'd worn when she went running, a hairbrush, a *People* magazine she'd bought and never gotten a chance to read.

Dad looked up at me like the smallest, most pathetic creature on the face of the Earth. "I'm sorry," he said, snuffling back his tears. "It's just . . . I just had this thought that I'm putting her in a box again."

Well, that was it for me. Boom—instant waterworks. I kind of slumped down on the floor and cried, and Dad scooted over to me and put his hand on my shoulder. "I hope you know," he said in this calm voice, because apparently me losing my shit helped him find his, "that I love Carmen, and I am excited about this new life we all get to have together, and that every single day of my life, your mom's absence is a knife in my heart. It's not something I will ever forget or get over. You understand? It's a scar on my soul. So I don't . . . I don't want you thinking I'm forgetting her. I will never forget her. Never."

Well, that was a hell of a speech, but I wasn't convinced. "Then why are you doing this?" I asked.

"Because I love Carmen, because I love the child we're having together, and because . . . because I'm still alive."

I stood up because that just sounded so disloyal to Mom that I couldn't stand being in the same room with him. "It's not like she wanted to die, Dad. It's not like she ran off with another guy or something."

"Don't you think I know that? What the hell do you want from me, Declan? Do you want me to spend the rest of my life moping in my room and listening to black metal and thinking about what used to be? Well, I'm sorry, but I'm not going to do that. I know your mom didn't choose to die, but I also know that she loved us too much to want us to be miserable for the rest of our lives."

I couldn't really come up with any kind of speech to match that. So instead I just said, "You suck," and left the room.

We didn't talk for two days after that, except for "Hand me a Phillips-head screwdriver" or "I need a three-sixteenth drill bit"—whatever kind of stuff was necessary to get little fix-it jobs done at the new house. Dad must have been pissed at me, too, because he wasn't even trying to teach me about what he was doing. I guess he figured I could pick it up by watching and helping, but he wasn't going to give me any instruction.

I was glad when the weekend came and I could head off to Sarah and Lisa's house. Because I wasn't mad at them; they were actually providing some stability in my life instead of turning everything upside down. So of course I sulked around their house and generally acted like a dick all weekend. It was weird—sometimes I felt like I could stand outside myself and see me being a dick, and I knew I should stop, but I didn't know how. I felt horrible, and I had no idea how to feel better.

Sunday night Dad and I had our big reunion, and I guess he was feeling like enough time had passed that we could make up or something.

"Hey," he said when I walked in the door.

"Hey," I said.

"Are we okay?" he asked.

"I don't know, Dad. I guess you are," I said, and went to my room. I mean, am I supposed to lie to the guy? I felt pretty far from okay. I guess I just felt like it was one thing if he was thinking with his dick and the little guy made him temporarily insane and he forgot about Mom for a while. I mean, I can sympathize with that. But to see him there doing his "Sympathy for the Devil" sobbing and to know that he hadn't forgotten Mom at all, and that he was marrying Carmen anyway—well, that just seemed a lot worse to me.

I thought about calling Neilly, since she was my only ally in this business, but really, she didn't have any idea what I was going through. Yeah, her life had been turned upside down and everything, but not like mine. She had a life I could literally only dream about. I mean, I used to have that dream all the time—that Dad and I were at the mall or something, and I'd catch this glimpse of Mom in the crowd, and I'd go running toward her, and she'd hug me, and I'd say, *I thought you were dead*, and she'd smile and say, *No, I'm not dead at all*, and I wouldn't even be mad about all the time when I'd thought she was dead, I would just be so relieved to see her that I would cry. And then I'd wake up all happy for about ten seconds, until I realized Mom was dead after all, and then I'd cry for real. So yeah, I don't think anybody with two living parents would have the first clue what the toxic stew in my brain was like.

The next morning I ate in silence and went to school. Neilly actually spoke to me briefly—we ended up in the lunch line together—and she said, "Hey, is your room done yet?"

"Yeah, the abattoir is almost complete. Unless you want the abattoir."

"What the hell is an abattoir?"

"It's a slaughterhouse. But I prefer the term killing floor."

She looked at me for a long moment. "You know, the fucked up thing is, that house is so creepy that I don't even know if you're joking."

I felt a little bad about being mean to the only person on Earth I could stand, so I said, "Yeah I'm joking. Actually, we spent the weekend working on the bathroom. New tile."

"Nice! You all packed up?"

"Not even close. You?"

"About halfway there. Well, listen, I guess I'll see you tonight."

"Tonight?"

"Yeah, you know. Youth group?"

Oh, I knew about youth group all right. But I had been in such a foul mood that I'd totally forgotten about it, and if I had remembered, I would have decided to blow it off. But if Neilly was going to be there, well, it might be worth going through the corny-ass get-to-know-you games one more time.

That afternoon I went to church to do some work before youth group. Despite my best efforts to clean up the parish hall after coffee hour on Sunday, I can't really say I get every single crumb of coffee cake that gets spilled in there, which means I have to be especially vigilant about the rodent control. So the last thing I do before I leave on Sunday is slip on some latex gloves, bait some snapping mousetraps with peanut butter, and set them around everywhere.

So on Monday afternoon I have to do corpse patrol. This

Monday was a pretty good haul—two adults and three juveniles. I bagged them up, washed my hands, and went to see Sarah and Lisa, who were opening cartons of Chinese food in Sarah's office.

"Hey," Lisa said, "Mr. Sunshine. Want some Kung Pao Chicken?"

I take a lot of shit from Lisa. I don't know why. There's something about the way she delivers it that makes it easier to take from her than it is from Dad or Aunt Sarah. I weighed the impact of Kung Pao Chicken on my breath against my hunger and the inherent metalness of a dish packed with dried hot peppers.

"Got any mints? 'Cause that Kung Pao Chicken is smelling fantastic, but you know, it can be kind of close quarters there in the old youth group, and I don't want my breath to send any of the lovely young ladies running for the exits."

Sarah rolled her eyes. "Dec, you know youth group is not some meat market. It's supposed to be a place where you guys can get in touch with your higher selves, not some kind of kegger with prayers."

Lisa punched Sarah on the arm. Maybe this was why I took so much shit from Lisa—she dished it out equally and usually gave a lot more to other people than she did to me. "You're full of shit," she said to Sarah.

Sarah sputtered. "I—I am not . . ."

"Didn't something important happen on a youth group retreat when you were fifteen?" Lisa asked.

Thankfully, Sarah jumped in with, "That is not something we're discussing in front of Declan—"

"And you and I met at a social justice conference," Lisa said. "I think it was after the keynote speech that we—"

I had to put a stop to this. Like I said, I had begun to think of Lisa and Sarah in parental terms, which meant I never wanted to know anything about them having sex. "Whoa, Lisa, I really appreciate your pointing out the hypocrisy, but I'm gonna have to side with Sarah here about not hearing the details. I mean, no offense."

"None taken. Ingrate. Eat your Kung Pao. And yes, I have mints for you. All I was trying to point out was that spirituality and sexuality can coexist. In fact, they always do, and it's kind of silly to pretend that our spiritual selves don't live in bodies with hungers and urges."

"Uh, yeah. Listen, I'm sorry, but I wonder if you could just not say the word *urges*. It kinda grosses me out. No offense."

Lisa rolled her eyes. Sarah ate an egg roll and smiled.

Neilly and I sat next to each other in the circle when youth group started and made jokes when Sarah said something unintentionally sexual. It was nice for a couple of reasons. One, of course, was that I was making sex jokes with a hot girl. Although, strangely, now that I was closer to Neilly, scoring with her seemed even more impossible than it had when she didn't even know my name. The other was that it was just nice to feel like I was part of something. Like I had something to belong to.

So youth group was going better than it ever had, and then

it suddenly got even better. Chantelle—the hot, bespectacled genius from my math class—came in looking kind of scared. I wanted to run over to her and throw my arm around her and tell her that anybody with a rack like hers was always welcome here, but Sarah did a much better job of dispensing the reassuring welcomes than I ever could, so I left it to her. It took her a minute to say hi, though, because I guess she was noticing, and being appalled by, me scoping out Chantelle.

When it was time for us to put blindfolds on and hold hands, I did a really half-assed job tying mine on so I could see out the bottom if I tilted my head back. So when Sarah steered me over to somebody with really soft hands, I leaned my head back and saw Chantelle, with her light brown skin, her amazing chest, and her glasses over her blindfold. That was so cool. I don't know what it is with the glasses—I guess when I see a girl wearing glasses, I think it means she might have a brain in her head, though maybe she doesn't, and I also think it means that she's comfortable enough with who she is that she's not trying to hide behind contacts. Of course, maybe it just means she has a weird prescription that they don't make contacts for. In any case, Chantelle was wearing her glasses over her blindfold, and I nearly fainted she was so freaking cute.

I looked over at Sarah. She was looking right at me, so I guess I was busted on the whole not looking thing. I mouthed the words *thank you* at her, and she smiled at me and flipped me the bird, which made it really hard not to crack up—actually it was pretty good revenge on her part, I had to hand it to her.

While I was at it, I peeked around to see who Neilly was paired up with. I hated him instantly. Mostly because you could tell even through the blindfold that Neilly was making goo-goo eyes at him. And then there were the other problems. For one thing, he had long hair, but his was all rock-star edgy instead of long and limp like mine. Also, he was tall and good-looking and not deathly pale. Oh yeah, and he was wearing a Motorhead T-shirt. I don't know if this kid even knew that, but still, it indicated that he was a little darker, and perhaps weirder, than your average Jocky McMoron. If she was there swooning over some short-haired jock in a football jersey or something, then at least I could write it off as like, well, she's into guys like that. But here she was going into heat over a long-haired metal guy! Sure, he was taller and better-looking than me, but still.

Once she'd finished with the obscene finger gestures, Aunt Sarah started her spiel about judging people, and how we should find something we had in common with the person across from us. Since Chantelle was obviously feeling shy, I decided I should start.

"Uh," I said, "so, let's see. Something we have in common." I racked my brains thinking about what I knew about Chantelle other than that she was good at math. I decided I didn't know anything else about her, so I might as well just be honest about myself. Kind of a weird strategy that most guys avoided, and probably a really dumb idea in my particular case, but it's not like I had been having tons of success with the ladies in any case. "Um, I'm good at school, but I hate it anyway." True, and probably the perfect balance of good boy/bad boy that the ladies craved.

There was this long pause. Bad move. Terrible move. Finally, she said in her voice that was almost as soft as the skin on her hands, "Me, too. I'm really good at math, but I hate school."

"Yeah. I could almost deal with the teachers trying to suck every last ounce of creativity out of my brain, if it weren't for the evil morons who run the social side of stuff."

She laughed a little bit. I was so in! "It's pretty hard to find a way to fit in. Especially when . . . well, when you're obviously different."

"Yeah. I mean, for me, it's my sexiness. You know, the guys are jealous, the girls are intimidated, and so that leaves me kind of isolated."

Now she laughed aloud. "So if I took off this blindfold right now, I'd be intimidated by your sexiness?"

"Totally. It's actually pretty terrifying the first time you encounter it."

"Are you sure you're not just really weird?"

"Well, I guess that's another possibility. But my version is a lot more fun." I leaned my head way back and peeked at her, smiling. So far so good, but there was a crucial step missing here that I didn't really know how to get past. Namely, how do you go from making them laugh to making out? Well, maybe my new sister could help me figure that one out.

But when Neilly grabbed me at the end of the meeting, all she could talk about was how horny she was for some guy she'd seen at the beginning of group. This was problematic for me in so many ways. For one, that guy wasn't me. For another, he wasn't me. And so on and so on, not to mention the fact that she failed to explain how I could engender those same lusty feelings in Chantelle. From start to finish, the conversation was a total loss.

Neilly gave me a ride home, and there was a note from Dad on the kitchen table. *Dec—I am at the new place doing some painting. Back by 10. If I don't see you, make sure you clear the decks for tomorrow afternoon. You and I have a family therapy appointment.*

Oh, for God's sake. I freeze the guy out for one weekend, and now we have to go talk about our relationship. If it weren't for the fact that he'd recently impregnated a woman, I'd have to wonder if Dad were turning into one.

This I could call Neilly about.

"Guess what?" I said as soon as she picked up the phone.

"You know the identity of the mystery hottie, and you're calling me on three way?"

Oh, for the love of SuicideGirls. Neilly Foster just said "three way."

"You wish. No. Get this. I mean, of all the horrible surprises

I've gotten recently, this has to be the worst. Guess where Dad and I are going tomorrow after school?"

"Family therapy?"

"No, it's . . . Oh, wait. Yeah. That's right. Fucking family therapy. Can you believe that? Wait, how'd you guess that?"

"Because Mom and I are going on Thursday."

CHAPTER EIGHT
Neilly

FAMILY THERAPY, WHAT A BUNCH OF HORSESHIT. WE don't need some PhD to tell us we have problems. That's already more than apparent from the way my mom has been alternately following me around like a puppy needing approval and then yelling at me for not reacting the way she must have wanted me to.

For some random reason, she seems to think I enjoy being miserable. What she doesn't understand is that none of this is any better for me than it is for her. I wish more than anything we could just go back to the way things were. Unfortunately, the sudden appearance of Dec's dad means nothing's the same, and nothing will ever be the same again.

Because you know what they say—three's a crowd. Whenever I'm at home, it seems like it's always Mom, Dec's dad, and me. Guess who's the odd one out in that scenario?

And I can tell it's only going to get worse once we all move into that House of Horrors. Because if three's a crowd, I'm sure all five of us—Mom, Dec's dad, me, the unnamed spawn of Mom and Dec's dad, and Dec (who recently informed me his bedroom in the new digs has a history of bloodshed, creepier even than my mom getting it on with Dec's dad)—will be a freaking riot. Or something equally as loud and unsettled. And I don't mean that in a good way.

It's just that, no matter how hard I try, I can't get over the fact that my mom was carrying on this secret double life behind my back. I mean, why couldn't she have started by telling me she was thinking about dating again and then eased me into the rest of it—rather than dating, having unprotected sex, getting impregnated, and making plans to get married, all without ever peeping a word of it to me until I found her naked with her aging lover boy?

The thought of that day still makes me want to gouge my eyes out with a newly sharpened pencil. I probably feel the same way clueless parents do when they find out their straight-A student is, like, running a crystal-meth lab from their basement, or their super-religious-I'm-gonna-stay-a-virgin-until-I'm-married high school senior pops out a baby between dances at the prom. Like, *How could I have been so blind?*

"So, how do you two *feel* about all these *changes* in your *life*?"

Dr. Rappaport was straight out of an *SNL* skit, peering at us over smart-looking glasses perched on the end of her nose, pen poised and ready to scribble about how crazy we both were on the pages of the notebook resting on her crossed legs, using that low, soooooothing tone of voice. If I hadn't been so irritated about having to be there in her office, I would've laughed.

Instead, I examined my very bitten-up nails.

"I feel very excited, of course," my mom jumped in when she realized I wasn't slobbering all over myself to offer up a peek into our personal lives. "But I also feel like it has driven a wedge between Neilly and me, and that, of course, makes me feel dreadful."

I just sat there, not saying a word, while my mom stared at me expectantly. Dr. Rappaport finally interjected herself into the quietquietquiet of the room.

"Neilly, it sounds as though your mom is experiencing a roller coaster of emotions. Is that how you feel, too?"

I stared at the doodles I'd added to my black Converse. On the toe of my right shoe, I'd crossed out *Neilly + Sam* and written *cheating fuckface* instead.

My mom jumped all over my nonreaction. "See? She's like this all the time lately. Completely uncommunicative."

I rolled my eyes while my mom dabbed at hers with a Kleenex. This was going nowhere fast.

"As well as angry and sarcastic," she added. "It started with the divorce, but it's gotten worse since Thomas and I met."

I glared at her. More like since she'd met Dec's dad, didn't tell me she'd met him, started banging him, got knocked up by him, and decided to marry him without even telling me she'd met him. It was so messed up. How could she not *see* that?

"Let's try putting your frustrations into words, Neilly," Dr. Rappaport told me. "Give them a voice."

If the fake doctor wanted a voice, I didn't want to let her down. So I launched into my best impression of my mom. "This is going to be a great adventure for all of us, Neilly! You'll have the big family you always wanted!"

My mom glowered in my general direction, and I went back to being plain old me. "I have no say in any of this, no matter what voice I put on my frustrations. So what's the point? Let's just agree to disagree."

After the family therapy debacle, we pretty much didn't talk to each other for the rest of the week and on through the weekend. Not that it could've upset my mom too much—she spent all her free time with Dec's dad at the House of Horrors, trying to see through the mold and grime enough to figure out how she was going to decorate the behemoth. I could've cut to the chase and made it easy for her—a creepy old pipe organ here, Dracula's coffin over there, hellhounds in the mudroom. See? Piece of cake.

Sad to say, though, even my mom had a better social life than I did by this point.

Going to parties hadn't seemed all that appealing lately. Yelling over loud music just to make conversation, and then realizing the conversation was completely ridiculous because everyone else was drunk and I was stone-cold sober . . . I guess it all just seemed like way too much effort without Sam and Lu. So my life had turned into pretty much just school and home. All alone.

I started to think that maybe parties had never been much fun.

Or that maybe *I* had never been much fun.

Or maybe both.

It was hard to tell at this point.

All I knew for sure was that by Monday night, I was practically salivating to get to Aunt Sarah's church youth group. It was the most social thing—no, make that the only social thing—I'd done since the disaster of a party with foamy-lipper Tanner McManus, unless you counted looking at random people's Facebook photos six thousand times without ever commenting on any. And if that didn't make me a big fat loser with a capital BFL, I didn't know what did.

Still, that didn't stop Hermit Girl—aka me—from arriving way too early to even pretend to have an ounce of cool left. Jumping the gun so heavily would've normally left me hanging out all alone at the church for a good half an hour, but luckily Dec was already there doing a little cleaning up.

"Whoa, brother, that's a mighty big broom you've got there," I called out to him.

"That's what she said," he shot back, grinning. "So how was family therapy?"

"The biggest time waster on the planet," I said. "You?"

He plunked himself down next to me. "Same."

"You know what the real kicker is, Dec?"

"No, what?"

"It's not even that I'm mad about my mom falling in love with your dad, or them having a baby, or that crazy creepfest of a house—though I'm sure that's what therapist lady wanted me to say."

"It isn't?"

"Not really. I'll totally beat you if you tell anyone this, but sometimes I actually think that part might be a tiny bit fun. You know, moving into a bizarro new house, having a bizarro new baby brother to torture—"

"I thought you were convinced the evil spawn was going to be a girl," he interrupted me.

"I meant you," I teased, giving him a gentle elbow to the ribs.

"Funny. Ha. Like not at all."

"Seriously," I said. "The part that really bugs me is that my mom is acting so different. We used to be so close. Now we're like . . . I don't know . . . acquaintances or something."

"I know what you mean," he said, nodding in agreement. "It's like they forgot about everything that happened before they met or something."

"Maybe they turned into zombies?" I asked, only half kidding now.

"Yeah, love zombies. It really fits the ambience of the new digs, right?"

While we talked, kids finally started showing up. One here, one there, then in a steady stream. As they were filling up cups of Gatorade and soda, grabbing a handful of pretzels, then plopping themselves down on the carpet, I got down to the business of trying to spot hothothottie the second he came through the door.

"Crap, that's not him," I said every time someone who wasn't my fake Travis from We the Kings filtered in. And when it finally was him, I gasped to Dec, "Omigosh, he's waaay cuter than I remembered."

Dec was all scowly and silentsilentsilent. Then this: "You're supposed to be here to learn more about yourself and your relationship with God, not some kid you've never even talked to. How shallow can you be?"

Great. He'd gone from perfect, understanding half brother to shithead in the span of about three seconds. "How much of an asshole can *you* be?" I demanded, giving him my best Nerves of Steely Neilly look.

Dec opened his mouth two, three, four times before anything came out. "I just think you need to get your head straight before you bring another guy into your life, that's all."

So now Mr. Metal But Totally Should Be Emo Man was psychoanalyzing me? That was the last straw. I was *never* talking about my feelings again, to anyone. Not even—or should I say, most especially—my new stepbrother. "Thanks a lot, Freud, but I think I can handle my dating life without your expert input," I said, and stalked off to the complete opposite side of the room. I was too mad to even look at Mr. Hottie out of the corner of my eye.

"Listen up, people," Aunt Sarah was saying a minute later. "Tonight we're going to talk about the ingredients of a good relationship, and what happens when they're not present."

She started passing out blindfolds again. "Same rules as last time—no peeking, no identifying personal information, just heartfelt sharing. To be consistent, I'm going to pair you with the same person as last week."

Soon enough, Aunt Sarah plunked me down on the rickety old couch next to my partner and placed my hand in his. "Get talking, you two."

I had the exact same reaction as last time—the perfect fit, the feeling of being entirely at ease and comfortable with the guy. "So what do you think?" he asked.

"I guess truth is the most important thing there is," I said, thinking about the recent lack of it in my relationships with Sam, Lulu, and my mom, and how it had ruined everything. "Because without it, you're pretty much left with no relationship at all."

A long pause. Then, "I don't think you're left with nothing. I think you're just left with a messed-up relationship. Like if one person cheated and the other felt like they couldn't trust them anymore—"

"Has that ever happened to you?" I interrupted. Maybe it would be another thing we had in common.

"Not that I know of. You?"

Though I wanted him to think of me as a person no one would ever dream of cheating on, I felt like it would be really bad karma lying like that in a church. Especially after I'd spouted off about how important trust was to a relationship.

"Yeah," I admitted, my voice registering just above a little peep. "Yeah, it has. Recently." I had to use the old pinch-myself trick to stop from getting emotional. It was getting harder and harder to distract myself these days, and it was really starting to piss me off.

He squeezed my hand. "I'm sorry."

"Why?" I asked with a hoarse laugh. "It's not your fault."

We sat for a long while before he spoke up again. "Well, want to know what I think?"

"Shoot."

"I think honesty is important, like you said. But what I actually think is that the key to a good relationship is forgiveness, because without it we're all completely screwed."

Over the past few years, I'd become a total master at the art of *not* forgiving people—first the kids who'd given me shit about my dad, and now Sam, Lu, and my mom. In my head, that made me strong, not screwed. "Why do you say that?"

"Because we're all human, and we all make mistakes. Without forgiveness, we'd all be walking this Earth angry and alone, and I think that would really suck."

"So you think I should just forgive the asshole who cheated on me, and the used-to-be best friend he cheated on me with?"

"Yeah, it might be hard to believe, but I really think you should."

Was he kidding? No freaking way. "Why?"

"Because I don't want you to be angry and alone."

I drew in a sharp breath. I don't know what surprised me more—the realization that I'd just made, or that I was about to admit it to a total stranger. "I kind of already am."

"All the more reason, then."

"Time to wrap it up," Aunt Sarah called out before we could say anything else. "No more talking. Just silent thought and prayer while I lead you all back to your places. I heard a lot of conversation tonight about unconditional love, trust, faithfulness, even forgiveness, and I want to tell you you're on the right track. Fact is, all of those things are important. And they're also exactly what God brings to your relationship, and what you should give back in return. You can all take off your blindfolds now."

Once again, the hottie had disappeared, leaving me with all the notties. As everyone filed out of the room a little while later, Dec approached me, his eyes on the broom he was once again pushing around. "Neilly, I'm sorry for what I said before. It was stupid, and I know it was none of my business."

I held up my hand, ready to take the lesson I'd learned tonight and apply it to my own life. "Forgiven. And if it makes you feel any better, I'm going to listen to your advice and not go out of my way to try to meet that guy I was drooling over before."

Dec looked shocked. "Really? Why not?"

"I decided maybe he's just my proof that I can actually get over Sam." The thought had just occurred to me, and I liked how it kind of took the pressure off the situation. So I could still think a guy was hotter than hot. But as for a real relationship—that could come later, with someone else, sometime else, when my life was less of a mess.

"Makes sense," Dec said. "Now if I could only get over Chantelle, I'd be all set."

"The sizzling one?"

"That's her."

"Why do you have to get over her at all?"

Dec suddenly couldn't meet my eyes again. "I mean . . . she's not like all those other chicks I hang with. . . . You know, the metal ones . . . With them, I kind of just jump in for the kill when I want to . . . uh . . . get something started. But Chantelle, she's different. So it's probably better if I just back off."

I tried to keep a serious look on my face. I didn't believe there were a million metal chicks who came before Chantelle any more than I believed Dec's room in the House of Horrors had been a killing field, or whatever he'd told me. "Why don't you just make a move on her instead?"

"I told you, this girl's not like that."

"Dec, she's just a girl. And she'd be lucky to hang with a menacing metal guy like you, right? So don't worry—just go for it."

He looked like he'd rather be caught in one of his sexton mousetraps than be talking about this with me. "I don't know . . . ," he said, then trailed off, shaking his head.

"You mean, like, where to start?" I asked, filling in the blanks. "Just remember, a first kiss should never, ever involve tongue. It's got to be warm and soft, sweet and lingering. Lips not too dry, and definitely not too wet. Just get her laughing, and when she looks up at you and kind of tilts her head to the side, you know the time is right."

Dec laughed nervously. "No, I mean . . . how to get it right, I guess."

"Just do it," I said, and leaned over and gave him a sweet,

sisterly little smooch—on his cheek, mind you, my brain hadn't gone completely mushy, despite all this churchy stuff—to demonstrate exactly what I meant. "Like that. See?"

By now, he'd turned twelve thousand shades of crimson and gone mute. Then crimson quickly morphed to ghostly pale—like, more ghostly than usual, and before tonight I really thought that would be impossible. I worried that I might've actually embarrassed my poor vampire-stepbrother-to-be to death.

"Dec? Hey, Dec?" I said, holding out my fist for a little friendship power tap. "I didn't mean to freak you out. I was just trying to show you how it's done. Isn't that what wicked stepsisters are for? To teach you wicked stuff?"

He nodded, but didn't look so sure about it.

"And by the way, I'll be needing a favor in return," I told him. "So you're not forever indebted to me, know what I mean?"

"What kind of favor?" he croaked.

"Would you consider being my 'not date' at my dad's thing?" I asked, tossing out another crazy brainstorm I'd just had. "I have to show up with someone, and I'd rather not have it be a guy who's going to get the wrong idea. So what do you say? Do we have a deal?"

Dec finally found his voice again. "Deal."

Great. Now I wouldn't have to worry about being mistakenly

put into the same category as Roger's loser son Griffin, who was going dateless to the ceremony probably because he was still embarrassed about his awesome, awesome dad—and mine.

Screw him and his homophobic hang-ups. Dec and I would provide more than enough enthusiasm to make up for his lack of it.

CHAPTER NINE

DECLAN

WELL, I GOT OUR FAMILY THERAPIST FIRED AFTER one session. I honestly thought it was going to take three.

After we left the session, Dad said to me, "Well, that was a disaster. You were really embarrassing, Declan."

"What, just because I wouldn't talk?"

"No, because of the lecherous way you were looking at Dr. Rappaport." Hmmm. It's true that I had amused myself through the boredom and horror of our first family therapy session by imagining a private session with Dr. Rappaport, who looked like an even hotter Tina Fey, but I hadn't realized I was being that obvious.

"Well, I mean, Dad, it's not my fault the therapist is smokin' hot. What was I supposed to do?"

"Not stare at her legs when she was talking to you. That would have been a good start."

"Dad. I mean, I know you're engaged and everything, but have you looked at this woman?"

"Dec, there are conversational places where I just can't go with you. Your lustful feelings for a woman at least twice your age is definitely one of those places."

"But she is hot. You know it."

"Fine. She's an attractive woman. I'll make sure I find you a male therapist for your next session."

"What do you mean, for *my* next session? I thought this was a *we* thing!"

"Well, I just realized that having me there might actually be preventing you from saying whatever is on your mind, so it might be more helpful for you to go on your own for a while so you can get this stuff out without worrying what I might think about it."

"Dad, except for the part about Dr. Rappaport being an incredible hottie, that's the most sensible thing you've said in weeks."

"I never said Dr. Ra—"

"It was implied. Clearly implied."

Dad fought back a smile.

I was feeling pretty proud of myself until Dad told me the next day that Dr. Gordon had had a cancellation and we'd be heading straight over for my one-on-one therapy session. "Dad, I'd be totally happy to have a one-on-one with Dr. Rappaport. Actually, a two-on-one would be fine, too, because her receptionist—"

"Do you have any idea how horribly uncomfortable it makes me when you say stuff like that?"

"Duh. Why do you think I'm saying it?" It's true. Except for getting busted for BitTorrent porn, I had been concealing the fact that I am, as Lisa might say, "a sexual being" from Dad ever since I started feeling like a sexual being, and now I was flaunting it all over the place, mostly because I'd discovered it gave me power over him.

He stared at me for a minute.

"What?"

"You just— I dunno. Your mom had that same stubborn, mischievous streak. It makes it really hard for me to stay mad at you about it."

Touché—I make Dad uncomfortable by talking about my desires; he makes me uncomfortable by talking about Mom. I don't know if he's doing this intentionally or not. In either case, I don't respond, but I really like hearing that there's part of Mom surviving in me, so I smile, which, of course, means Dad wins.

And then he won again, because I wound up crying in Dr. Gordon's office. I swear I don't know how the guy did it. It might have had something to do with him being this really unattractive white-haired old man, so I couldn't be distracted by thinking about him naked. In fact, the very thought of that is completely horrifying—it probably looks like a Cannibal Corpse album cover or something.

But so, somehow, and I don't really remember how, I ended up spilling all the beans, the beans I'd been mostly keeping to myself, about how much I missed Mom, and how, even though Dad drove me nuts sometimes, I really liked it when it was him and me against the world, the horrible, awful world that kills a kid's mom when he's nine. Now Dad was going back into the world, which left just me on the outside.

Oh yeah, not to mention the fact that his knocking up her mom had totally ruined my chances of ever banging Neilly Foster. Okay, it's not like I ever had a chance to bang Neilly Foster anyway, but it was almost harder—really, if you know what I mean—to be close to her all the time and talk to her and stuff and know that it was never ever going to happen. Before, she was like some Victoria's Secret model or something—well, I never got to see her in her underwear, but what I mean is that she was someone who basically lived in my fantasy life and not the real world at all.

"Eh," Dr. Gordon said, "so there's a beautiful girl you never get to have. Nobody gets to have them all. And once you're married—forget it. The stuff about your dad—that I get. The stuff about your mom that you're hinting at but not really saying—I get that, too. But the hot stepsister—no big deal. You'll go into the bathroom after she defecates one day, and she won't be some airbrushed fantasy figure anymore, and you'll go find somebody you can actually date."

"Neilly Foster has never defecated in her life." I mean, really— a beautiful girl like that squatting and laying some cable—it's so absurd I couldn't even picture it.

"If that were true, she'd have quite the distended abdomen," Dr. Gordon said. "Also, she'd be dead. I don't think either of those is true."

"'Distended Abdomen' would be a good name for a band," I told him.

"Yeah, well, send me some royalties when you hit it big. For now, our fifty minutes are up, so get out of here. I'll see you next week."

"All right," I said. What a dick. I liked him.

The ride home was fun because I could see Dad dying to ask what happened, knowing it was inappropriate to ask what happened, and finally giving in and asking, "So how was it?"

"It was okay. We just talked about shit," I said, and I smiled to myself because Dad would probably never guess that shit was an actual topic of conversation.

Youth group turned out to be another holding-hands-with-Chantelle session, but I was not my usual glib and charming self. I was tired from crying, and also once you unlock that box in your brain where you keep all the hurt, it's not that easy to shut it again.

"So," Chantelle said, "what makes a good relationship?"

"Nobody dying," I said, and realized only too late that I'd just snapped at a hot girl. What the hell was wrong with me?

"Whoa. That's cheery. Are you being ostracized for your sexiness again?"

"No, I just . . . I . . . Do you ever have, I mean, can you . . . I'm sorry, I can't even put a freaking sentence together. I feel like something a dog puked up, licked up, and shat out."

"Nice image."

"Sadly accurate image. If you had just the glasses without the blindfold, you'd see I'm right."

"How do you know I wear glasses?"

Crap. I just gave myself away. Well, I figured I might as well just lay it all out, then. "Uh. I peeked. I'm sorry."

"You peeked? That's bad."

"Sorry."

"No, you're not." I wasn't peeking now, but I could hear the smile in her voice.

"Yeah, okay, I'm not. I mean, I . . . ugh, I'm sorry. It's hard for me to play the game here tonight because I'm just all messed up from thinking about stuff that makes me sad."

"Do you want to, like . . . I mean, I know we don't really know each other, but if you want to tell me . . ."

"I appreciate it, but I don't know if I can do it without— I mean, I'm kinda holding it together right now, and I don't think I can stand it coming apart, if you know what I mean."

"Yeah. I do, actually."

A lightbulb went off in my head. "Hey, maybe this is like really cheesy or whatever, but, I mean, I like talking to you, and maybe I could, like, buy you a cup of coffee or something to thank you for putting up with me being such a mess tonight. Like tomorrow after school?"

"Sure. How will I know it's you, though?"

"I guess you're going to have to peek."

She pulled one wonderfully soft hand out of mine, and we each used our free hand to pull the blindfolds down off our eyes. Of course, I had already looked at her, but I did need to check to make sure she didn't scream in horror when she looked at me. It occurred to me that the black Demonic Stain shirt might not have been the best choice of attire for tonight.

Chantelle didn't scream. She just looked, smiled, and put her blindfold back on as Sarah barked, "No peeking!" at us. "Okay," Chantelle said, "you don't actually look like dog shit, no matter how you feel, and I think I'm going to be able to withstand your sexiness, so yeah, I'll have coffee with you."

So that's how you do it. It occurred to me that I may have just grown a pair, metaphorically speaking. What's weird is that I'm sure I had been able to do it only because I was in a grumpy, screw-the-world, I-don't-care kind of mood. Maybe I should do that more often. "I'm glad, because, you know, a lot of people—"

"Find you intimidating. I know. You'd better have a new joke next time."

"Got it. I'll work on my material."

Once we got back in our little sharing circle, I couldn't look at Chantelle. I also couldn't look away from her. This presented some difficulties. Fortunately, Sarah just yakked and then dismissed us without forcing us to share our feelings, which was good: mine seemed to involve a tremendous sense of excitement mixed with gut-wrenching panic, because, of course, once Chantelle saw me for who I really was, she'd be horrified, and then I'd have something else to be sad about, and, I mean, I know next to nothing about girls, but I do know that hanging your hopes on a teenage girl's affections is a pretty dumbass thing to do. But I was doing it anyway.

Or, at least I was until Neilly freaking kissed me after youth group. I mean, yeah, it was a kiss on the cheek, kinda sisterly, I suppose, but she's not my sister. Not yet, anyway.

If I can just . . . I mean, what the hell was she trying to do to me? I think she was trying to help me, but oh my God, it didn't help. And assuming things went well with Chantelle, how exactly would I explain my whereabouts when I escort Neilly to her dad's wedding? "Uh, yeah, I can't go out tonight. . . . I have to take my sister to her dad's wedding to Roger, the UFC guy. And before you ask, Yes, I will be attempting to cop a feel in the limo." No, that won't do at all.

Alone in my room later, I face a masturbatory dilemma. Neilly Foster, whose lips, let's not forget, touched my skin tonight, and who I really shouldn't be thinking about like that anymore, in some kind of off-the-shoulder little black cocktail dress, preferably with a pentagram or upside-down cross hanging into her cleavage, or Chantelle, clad only in glasses? My phone rings—well, actually growls, since I've got a Dimmu Borgir ringtone—and the screen tells me it's Neilly calling, and it would just be too creepy to follow through while I'm actually on the phone, so I zip up and answer.

"Sis. What's up?"

"Hey. I know you probably know this anyway, but I just want to make sure you're . . . I mean, you know, I don't want to be a bitch about you doing me a favor, but you're not going to like—"

"Wear corpse paint and chains and bring a dead rodent to your dad's ceremony?"

"Well, I mean, not . . . I don't know what corpse paint is, but yeah. Part of the bargain here is that you kind of feign normalcy for the night."

"Deal. But you have to help me."

"I'm on it."

"So if I'm having coffee with her, like, first of all—"

"Mints. Strong ones. Coffee breath is not as bad as cigarette breath or garlic breath, but it definitely comes in third."

"What about onion breath?"

"Indistinguishable from garlic breath, so they count as the same thing."

"Got it."

"So make sure you pop a mint after your mochaccino. Gum won't do, in case there's tongue, but you have to let *her* initiate the tongue. If you go in for a kiss and jam your tongue down her throat, you're done."

"But she can jam her tongue down my throat?"

"Would you mind?"

"Are you kidding?"

"There you go. But she would. This is why you need an interpreter."

"Okay, but what the hell do I say to her? I mean, I was kind of all screwed up from therapy and feeling kind of, like, fuck it, which is the only reason I was able to ask her out in the first place. And how do I get from talking to kissing?"

"Just be yourself. Your real self, not the self you try to pretend to be."

"What do you mean?"

"I mean, you're not scary, you're never really going to be scary, and girls don't like scary anyway, so you may as well give up on scary and go for sweet."

"Sweet? Isn't that, like, the kiss of death?"

"No. 'Nice' is the kiss of death. Sweet is okay."

"This stuff is absurdly complicated. Okay, so let's assume I find something to talk about. I was thinking I could milk the dead mom thing for sympathy."

"Hmmm . . . tragic, sad . . . that might work, as long as you don't actually cry. You could cry in front of her in, like, a month or something, but not on your first date. But I'll tell you the best thing you can do. This is a closely guarded girl secret, so don't go sharing it everywhere."

"I got it."

"Just listen to her. Worry less about what you're going to say to her, and just think about what you want to hear from her."

"Okay. Let me see if I've got all this—you know what, I'm writing this shit down so I don't forget. Okay, don't be scary, be myself—but not the true, pervy version of myself—be tragic, listen, and bring mints. Anything else? How do I get to the kiss?"

"You'll feel it when the time is right. If there's this lull that makes you think you should kiss her, then kiss her. That's all I can say. There's no magical signature move that will get the kissing started. It's just got to happen."

"So, like, when you were with Jocky McMoron, it just kind of flowed naturally?"

Things got kind of quiet. "No. There was a cheesy signature move. But I didn't know it was a cheesy signature move until he tried it on my ex–best friend, Hoey."

"So I shouldn't use a cheesy move to get a kiss, even though they obviously work since you and your best friend both fell for the same one."

"That's about it."

Just when I thought I was understanding things, it all went to hell.

"All right. Thanks. I'm going online to order my powder-blue tux now."

"You're joking, right?"

"Yeah. Don't worry. I'll look normal, I promise."

"Great. See you tomorrow."

"Okay." We hung up, and I felt bad because there was something else I wanted to say, but I didn't know how to say it. And I would have felt like a dork calling back, so I just sent this text: *Thx. i think im gonna like having a sister.*

I felt like a complete idiot the second I sent it, so I was relieved a few seconds later when I got this in return: *Nu siblings r the only part of this that doesnt suck.*

Hello? I sent back. *Mansion o metal?*

Like i said, Neilly sent back, and that ended it for the night.

I barely slept because I was nervous about coffee with Chantelle. I was so buzzed on adrenaline that I didn't even feel the lack of sleep all day. The next day I actually, for the first time I can remember, kind of agonized over what to wear. I have a T-shirt that is navy blue instead of black, so I wore that, along with some jeans and my Doc Martens steel-toed shoes, which are kind of old school but which I think are damn cool and not as scary as the boots I usually wear. It wasn't a complete transformation, but it was noticeable.

Noticeable enough that Dad busted my balls about it at breakfast.

"Who is she?" he asked.

"Dad, what the hell are you talking about?"

"I'm talking about the fact that you're not wearing all black for the first time since I can remember, and boys don't just change up their look like that unless there's a girl involved. So who is she?"

"Dad, you know, I just felt like a change," I lied.

"Yeah. Okay. Whatever," Dad said, grabbing his briefcase and heading out the door. I sat at the table, slack-jawed. Dad just exited with, "Yeah, okay, whatever," which, as a teenager, should really be my prerogative. The whole world has gone nuts around here.

School happened, as it tends to, but I was pretty checked out except in math class, when I stared at Chantelle, who sits in front of me, the whole time. She actually participated in class, so I guess she didn't notice, though she did turn around at one point and caught me staring. She flashed me this smile that blinded me with its brilliance, and that pretty well wiped my brain clean for the next hour or so.

After school, I stood in front of school feeling dumb, and Chantelle walked out and looked adorable, not to mention hot, and suddenly I didn't feel stupid anymore.

"Ready for some coffee?" I asked.

"Absolutely. I'm going to need it if I'm going to stay awake through those five million math problems she gave us."

"Cool."

There was a painfully awkward pause, and then we started walking the two blocks to Queequeg's. I wanted to hold her hand so bad that my own hand was itching, but I didn't.

This was a decision I would later come to regret, because holding Chantelle's hand might have been a bright spot in what turned out to be a very dark afternoon indeed.

"Hey!" somebody yelled behind us. I didn't really pay any attention because somebody bellowing at you after school can only mean trouble, so I just kept walking and hoped it was somebody else's trouble.

No such luck.

"Goth kid!" the voice yelled, and so I knew it was trouble on the line with a call for me. Even though goth and metal are, like, totally different things, I wouldn't expect the average Linkin Park fan to know that. I sighed and kept walking.

"Is this a normal occurrence for you?" Chantelle whispered. I looked over at her, and she looked all tense and tight, and I got pissed off because I didn't want her to think that hanging out with me always entails potentially violent encounters with brain-dead jocks. I turned to face the voice.

"Hey," the jock twice my size bellowed at me, "is it true?"

"That your parents are first cousins? Almost certainly." This was dumb. I know that, when dealing with the species *Jockus roidrageus*, one should meekly agree with anything they say and not attempt to best them in any respect so as to avoid a beat down, but, I mean, the girl I liked and who I was trying to take on my very first date ever was standing next to me.

Chantelle snickered, but the red-faced jock advancing on me didn't even get it. "No, faggot. That you're taking Neilly to her dad's . . . you know . . . thing. . . ."

Ah, Christ. I mean, I was going to kind of spring this on Chantelle a bit later, after she'd succumbed to my charm. I guessed that this must be Neilly's ex, and that, furthermore, he was bored with her slutty ex-friend and was trying to get her back, and so now he was here to warn me away from her. Which wasn't really going to work because (a) I wasn't with her like that, and, of course (b) we were getting ready to move in together. Yeah, life is complicated.

"You're taking Neilly Foster on a date?" Chantelle asked.

"Well, yeah, sort of, but she's my sister."

"So you're dating your *sister*?" Chantelle asked, looking horrified.

"Stepsister, really. Well, not technically, but uh—" I was interrupted by a large, meaty hand grabbing my shirt.

"Hey, faggot. I asked you a question."

"See," I said. "Here's what's dumb about this. You're calling me a faggot while getting ready to beat me for stealing your girl, who, by the way, *isn't* your girl anymore since you cheated on her with her best friend, but anyway, if I was a faggot, you wouldn't really have anything to worry about, now, would you? Do you see how dumb this is?"

He didn't see. "You calling me stupid?"

"Well, that was the implication, yeah, but I guess drawing inferences isn't really a strength of yours, so yes, I am, in fact, calling you stupid, Stupid. Did you get it that time?"

Jocky's face reddened, and he said, "You are so totally dead." He pushed me really hard just to make sure I got his point, and I fell backward. In front of Chantelle.

I have been on the wrong side of enough of these encounters to know the script. The push, while technically an assault, was my opportunity to beg, or explain, or otherwise humiliate myself in order to escape more physical punishment, but by this point I was pretty pissed at the guy, and he might have outweighed me by, like, a hundred pounds and been at least six inches taller than me, but he neglected one detail.

I was wearing steel-toed shoes.

So rather than continue the dance that led to his fist in my face, I simply kicked Jocky McMoron in the knee as hard as I could. I suppose kicking is a pretty girly way to fight, but I prefer looking slightly effeminate and getting away to getting the shit beaten out of me like a man.

Jocky crumpled to the ground and started crying. "Aaaagh! Shit! Goddamn! You're dead! My future! My ride!"

I didn't really know what he was talking about, so I kicked him in the nuts to shut him up.

This caused him to vomit.

I turned back to Chantelle. "So," I said, "still want that coffee?"

She looked at me and at the jock with digestive acid and spit dripping from the corner of his mouth and then back at me.

"I'm gonna pass. See you in church," she said, and all but ran from me.

I walked home alone and wondered how I'd managed to screw this up so completely. Scary wasn't working—I couldn't pull it off and it was off-putting besides—so for the first time in years, I had aimed for sweet instead of scary, and for the first time ever, I had hit scary.

Shit.

CHAPTER TEN
Neilly

I ALMOST DIDN'T PICK UP WHEN MY CELL PHONE RANG. It was after school, Lulu was trying to get me to talk to her again, and I was going to miss my ride home with Leslie Mitchell's mom if I didn't leave right then and there. But it was Dec calling, and I knew it without even looking at the screen because he'd assigned himself some weird Cookie Monster ringtone.

This put me in a total quandary.

I was kind of, sort of, maybe even considering listening to what Lu had to say after thinking more about youth group guy's advice: if I didn't want to be any more alone and unhappy in this world than I already was, I was going to have to give the whole forgiveness thing a shot.

On the other hand, I had my new stepbrother reaching

out to me for what I could only assume was advice. Because according to my watch, he should have been kissing Chantelle by now. And if he was calling me, he obviously didn't have his lips on hers.

And then there was my only ride home waiting impatiently while my sore feet begged me just to hop in the car and ignore Lulu and Dec already.

"Just a sec," I said to Lulu, putting up an index finger and reaching for my phone while waving Leslie and Mrs. Mitchell away all at the same time. Lulu must've thought she'd struck out again. She sat down on the nearest bench with a defeated little plop as the Mitchells' blue minivan drove out of sight.

"Brother, this is not a good sign," I said into the phone. "You are supposed to be making out with your new babe, all sweet minty breath by this time, not calling me."

The sound that came from the other end was worse than the stupid song that had preceded it. It was sputtering and guttural and completely indecipherable, like something I'd expect our new house to spew at Halloween. "Dec, just try to breathe."

Still more scariness. Maybe humor would do the trick.

"Does this mean you finally got laid for real?"

That got a little chuckle.

"Thank God. I thought I'd lost you there for a second."

"Neilly, I need your help," he finally managed to choke out. "Can you come get me?"

I glanced over at Lulu, who was giving me total puppy dog eyes. "Can it wait?"

"Uh, I don't think so," Dec said. It sounded like he was about to cry again. Well, not cry as in the normal kind of cry, but something more along the lines of what our house's imaginary hellhounds might produce if they were upset over having to eat leftover corpse again instead of a fresh kill.

"Alrighty then. Queeqeeg's in fifteen?"

"Try the police station as fast as you can."

"What?" I yelped. "I told you to be sweet with Chantelle, not stupid!"

"Yeah, well, that would've worked great if your ex, Jocky McMoron, hadn't gotten in the way. What an asshole. Now he's fucked up my life along with yours."

"You're joking, right?"

"Nope. Not even close. I'm even stuck in a cell with him."

I could only imagine how scared Dec must be. And what an awful sight he must be if he'd truly had a run-in with my ex. Sam could probably beat the crap out of Dec with one pinky nail. "You okay?"

"What do you think?" he shot back.

"I just wanted to make sure you, like, wouldn't be leaving for the hospital or something before I get there," I told him.

"Listen, Neilly, I'm fine physically. It's Jocky who's in the cell right now, holding one ice pack on his knee and one to his balls, moaning like the biggest pussy in the world."

"So he turned into a little kitty cat, you're growling like a bloodthirsty hellhound, and the both of you are in jail?"

"Something like that. Just come quick, okay?"

"You got it."

I slid my phone shut and walked over to Lu. "I do want to talk, Lulu, but I just can't right now."

She slumped down farther than ever. It was like she had no bones left in her body.

"So I'll call you later, okay?" I was almost starting to feel a tiny bit sorry for her. It was a nice change from feeling sorry for myself all the time.

She shrugged. "I doubt it."

"No really, I will," I told her. "It's just that this is kind of an emergency. My friend's in a jam, and I need to go bail him out. So I better start walking now, or else he'll be stuck at the police station forever, and he's not in the best frame of mind to handle that. . . ."

Lu fished around in her purse and pulled out a furry Juicy Couture key chain. "I could drive you," she said, dangling the keys in front of her. "And we could talk in the car on the ride over. What do you say?"

"Um . . . ," I said, thinking it over for just a sec before deciding it couldn't hurt. "I guess so?"

As we were walking to the parking lot, Lu kept clearing her

throat. But every time I thought she was about to say something, nothing came out. And I wasn't sure where to start, either, so we were stuck with awkward silence.

Hopping into her new-old dumper car—a tiny, dented, rusty bucket of crap that smelled like old socks—she turned the key and cranked the stereo. Still no conversation between us. Finally, I couldn't take it anymore.

"Nice ride," I offered up.

"Yeah, it was my birthday present from my parents," Lu said, backing out without even looking. Luckily, we didn't hit anything.

"It's a wonder you didn't make it onto *My Super Sweet Sixteen*," I continued busting on her.

"Well, that's probably only because I just turned seventeen. Otherwise, MTV for sure would've recruited me," she bantered back.

And so on and so forth it went, us goofing on each other so we didn't have to talk about the big pink elephant in the car—what had happened with Sam and why I wasn't, before a few seconds ago, talking to either one of them.

Once we pulled into the police station parking lot and careened into an open space, I figured it was time to get real. "Lu, I need to tell you something. Things are about to get seriously awkward here."

She hung her head, apparently waiting for me to rip into

her. It so wasn't what I had in mind. "I can take it," she said. "In fact, I deserve it. Fire away."

The whole situation was so absurd it set me off into an inappropriate giggle fit. It was kind of like cracking up at a funeral—so wrong, given the setting, that the thing that got you laughing in the first place seemed even more hilarious. Lulu and me, best friends turned enemies turned I'm Not Sure What We Were Right Now, about to come face-to-face with the guy who had torn us apart. And then there was the added strangeness of having my death-metal stepbrother all pissed off in one corner of a jail cell while the tearing-us-apart guy was holding ice packs to various body parts in the other. It was going to be weirdweirdweird. And that's why, no matter how hard I tried, I just couldn't stop laughing.

Lu waited patiently for my hysteria to end. "Well, this wasn't what I expected," was all she could say.

When I finally regained my composure, I tried to explain. "It's just that . . . hee-hee . . . God, this is going to be so bizarre . . . ha-ha-ha-ha . . . My very skinny, very socially awkward stepbrother just beat the shit out of . . . how might I say it . . . 'our' boyfriend Sam . . . and now they're both in jail . . . and Sam's family jewels are freezing . . . and . . . ." I couldn't even finish. The ice pack on the balls—too freaking funny!

Lu didn't seem to share my warped sense of humor. "Yeah, about that," she said, doing that twirling-her-hair/

biting-her-fingernails combo. "Not that you want to talk about it, I'm sure, but he isn't now and never was my boyfriend. And if it makes any difference, I socked him right after he tried to make a move on me."

Huh? What in the hell were we fighting about then? "So you're saying you *didn't* make out with Sam when I was away in San Fran with my dad?"

Lulu scrunched up her nose. "Well, the thing is, there was a kiss. But only for, like, a second. And I totally didn't know it was happening until it was already over."

"Lu, I really don't get what you're trying to tell me here. Like, somehow you lost your mind that night? An alien ate your brain?"

"Something like that," she said. "And the alien's name was Jack. Jack Daniel's, actually."

Lu getting wasted was almost more disappointing to me than her kissing Sam. Back in ninth grade, we'd once downed an entire bottle of champagne together while my mom was working late. Then we drunk-dialed our crushes, made complete asses out of ourselves by making and posting a dopey video of us dancing in our underwear online, passed out, and woke up with splitting headaches/stomachaches that lasted an entire day. After that, we'd vowed never to be so stupid again. And now she'd gone back on her promise. "What? Why?"

She shrugged. "You weren't there, and I felt like kind of a

loser because I didn't know that many people at the party. So I figured a few drinks might give me some liquid courage, you know? And I guess deep down inside I also thought maybe me being a crappy drunk was just a fluke."

"I take it it wasn't such fluke?"

"Not so much. I'm still a crappy drunk," she admitted. "Like, after a few shots, I decided it would be a good idea to go chill on the hammock in Crane's backyard until I sobered up. Needless to say, it made me totally seasick."

I was having a very hard time staying mad at Lu, and tried to remind myself she'd screwed up big-time. "Ha! Remember when you got motion sickness on the Ferris wheel at Six Flags during our seventh-grade field trip and you had to go to lie down at the first-aid station for the rest of the day?"

"Don't remind me," she said with a laugh. "Anyway, next thing I know, Sam plunks himself down next to me, which of course rocks the hammock even more, and he starts blahblahblahing about how he doesn't want to disappoint you or his parents, and he doesn't know what to do about your dad's ceremony—"

"I can totally see him doing that," I said, interrupting her story yet again. Sam couldn't make a decision to save his life, and he tended to stress himself out even more by going over his options a million times.

"Right. Well, I really wasn't feeling well and just wanted

to be left alone by this point, so I told him to go suck it like a juice box. Only he must've thought I asked him to go suck face or something, because suddenly he's all like, 'Wow that's really tempting, but I love Neilly, so I can't, sorry.' I had no idea what he was talking about, and I couldn't deal with his drunken babbling anymore, so I closed my eyes and prayed he'd go find someone else to be his therapist."

"We should totally make T-shirts that say SUCK IT LIKE A JUICE BOX and sell them at school for beaucoup bucks," I said, thinking out loud. About a future that included my BFF in it.

Lulu must've picked up on it, because she broke out into a huge grin. "Yeah, let's do that. So anyway, the next thing I know, Sam is saying, 'Fuck it, I'm not married' and shoving his tongue down my throat. Which was not a good idea for so many reasons—besides the fact that he's going out with my best friend, I already had the spins, and you know how sensitive my gag reflex is. . . ."

"No way! No way!" I screeched. I had a pretty good idea of how this story was going to end.

"Uh-huh," she said, confirming my suspicions. "First I punched him, then I puked on him. Right in his lap. Serves the asshole right."

"Yes, it does," I agreed.

In my head, though, I was also thinking how it was slightly redeeming that Sam hadn't just jumped at the chance to scam a hottie like Lulu—he'd at least had a little moral dilemma about it first. I mean, he hadn't actually *done* the right thing, but it had at least crossed his mind. "Why didn't you tell me any of this before?"

"Suzy had already told you everything you needed to hear," she said. "You didn't want to listen to any more crap, and I don't blame you."

"She did seem to enjoy seeing me freak out in the bathroom that day," I said. "So is this the end of partier-puker Lu?"

She nodded. "I just got ungrounded for the whole thing yesterday, and I think it's pretty safe to say I'll never drink again."

"Promise?" I asked, holding out my hand for a pinky swear.

"Promise," she said, locking her little finger onto mine. "Hey, Neilly, I'm really sorry about everything, you know? I love you."

"I forgive you," I said. It wasn't nearly as hard to do as I'd expected. "And I love you, too. Sorry I wouldn't listen to your side of things."

"No need to be sorry," Lu told me. "I was a total idiot."

I opened my door, stood up, then leaned back inside the car. "Well, aren't you coming with me?"

Lu looked up at me wide-eyed. "Really?"

My smile started at one ear and went all the way to the other. "I seem to have a soft spot for drunken assholes and idiots. Besides, you already told me a million times it won't happen again, and I don't think you're a liar along with all your other problems." She hopped out of the car, locked the doors, and then proceeded to punch me in the arm, not so softly.

"Do you really think someone's gonna try to steal that piece of shit?" I asked, running toward the police station before Lu could land another punch. "The key chain is worth more than the car!"

She ran after me, and a second later, we were laughing together like it was the old days.

Inside, things weren't quite as funny. After explaining I was there to bail out my "brother," the cop asked for my ID and then informed me that (a) we weren't really related, (b) I wasn't old enough to bail out anyone, and (c) it was going to cost me $1,000 I didn't have.

"Can I at least talk to him?" I pleaded.

"Be my guest," he said, nodding toward the cell. It was more like a sterile waiting room than Alcatraz, with a few plastic chairs and a built-in desk. I guess I shouldn't have been surprised. It wasn't like we lived in the 'hood, despite what you'd think if you saw the House of Horrors.

I found Dec sitting on one of the chairs, head in his hands. Sam and his icy balls were nowhere to be found.

"What am I gonna do with you, bro?" I asked through the bars.

Dec looked up and shook his head miserably. "Don't know. Things just got even worse. Jocky's father wants to press charges."

Sam's dad was a lawyer, like mine. "Hence the thousand bucks I can't possibly come up with, even if I was eighteen. Did you call your dad yet?"

"I'm trying to avoid it," he said. "We've been through a lot of crap lately, and I just don't think I can take any more of his trying to see into my soul."

"So what's your plan then?"

Dec shrugged.

"I'll call my dad, okay?"

"Whatever."

I got right through to my father this time, gave a short little explanation of our dilemma, and he said he'd be right over. And when I got back to Dec and Lulu, they were deep in conversation about Pungent Stench. "So you two discovered you both have horrendous body-odor issues while I was gone? And you like to talk about it?"

Lulu laughed. "It's a band."

Dec was certainly in a much better mood than when we'd arrived. "One of my latest and greatest discoveries," he informed me.

"Since when are you into metal?" I asked Lu.

"Apparently we have a lot of catching up to do," she told me.

I raised an eyebrow at her.

"Hey, you got a new stepbrother while we weren't speaking; I developed a new love for metal. It all makes sense," she told me.

I crossed my arms and waited some more.

"Fine. If you must know, my sister's new boyfriend is into it, and I guess I kind of like it."

Before I could ask her some seriously pertinent questions like "Why?" and "What have you been smoking?" my dad appeared.

"I want you to know, I don't approve of violence, Declan," he said through the bars. "Nice to meet you, by the way."

"I don't usually, either," Dec said, shaking my dad's hand. "Nice to meet you, too. Thanks for coming."

"It's never the answer to your problems, and I want you to promise me you'll remember that next time someone tries to push your buttons," my dad said, continuing with his lecture.

"I'll keep that in mind," Dec told him.

"Great. Just give me a second to get this all worked out, and then we can call your father together and explain what happened, okay?"

Dec nodded. He looked like maybe he wished he'd just called his own dad in the first place. Oh well. Too late now.

Before my dad went to talk to the cops, I gave him a big squeeze. "Thanks so much for helping us out, Daddy. I really appreciate it."

"Anytime, Neilly," he said, adding in my ear, "but you owe me. Big-time."

I figured he was right, so I didn't bother arguing. "Gotcha, Dad."

CHAPTER ELEVEN

DECLAN

"SO WHY'D YOU DO IT?" DR. GORDON ASKED.

"Because the guy was being a total dick, and it was the first chance I had to impress this girl, and he was just being so stupid—"

"Yeah, that I get. He humiliated you in front of a girl you liked. And he was stupid and violent, and you had to prove your superiority by being stupid and violent, too."

"Well, okay, it sounds dumb when you say it like that." I paused for a minute. "I guess that's because it's dumb, huh?"

"Your words," Dr. Gordon said, smiling. I really liked this guy. And I kind of wanted to deck him. "But that's not what I was asking about. I'm asking why you called your—whoever the hell this guy is to you instead of your father."

"Technically, it was Neilly who called him."

"Technically, you're being an asshole. Answer the question."

"Are you allowed to call me names like that? I mean, is that professional behavior?"

"File a complaint. Answer the question."

"I just—I just didn't want to deal with having a big conversation about my feelings and my mom and all that shit. I just knew, like—I mean, guys get into fights when girls are involved. It's not like some huge big unusual deal, right?" Gordon stayed silent. "But I knew Dad would want to have some big-deal conversation, and I just didn't friggin' feel like it right then, and Neilly said her father could get me out with no questions asked, and that sounded like a better deal than I was going to get from Dad, okay?"

Dr. Gordon sat and looked at me for a long minute. "It's a good story," he finally said, "but I'm not buying. I think you wanted to hurt your dad, provide a little payback for all the surprises he's sprung on you, so you reached out to a surrogate father and humiliated your own."

I sat on that for a minute. "I don't know. Maybe. I guess I'm still pissed at him."

I get why Dad wants me to go to therapy. I always go in there feeling nice righteous anger and come out feeling guilty. So when Dad picked me up, the first thing I said was, "Sorry."

"Dec, it's okay. I mean, I'm worried about you, of course, but who hasn't gotten into trouble over a girl?"

Ah, he wasn't gonna make this easy. "I mean, I'm sorry for calling Neilly's dad instead of you, okay?"

Dad looked over at me, his eyes moistening. "Thanks. I know you're pissed about everything right now, but I can't lose you, you know? Not yet. I still— I don't know if you really know how you got me through the time after Mom died, and—"

Cripes. This is exactly why I didn't want to talk to him. Mom this, Mom that. "Yeah, Aunt Sarah's told me, and it's not a subject I really want to get into right now."

"Yeah, okay, fine. But just know that that time in our lives, as awful as it was, is a bond between us that I will always treasure."

A bond that he will always treasure. I was being raised by a human greeting card.

"That's great. Can we get some Chinese food?"

"You know what? I would love that." So we did.

The air stayed clear for a few days, and we had our meeting with our court-appointed mediator, since Dad (and not Neilly's dad, I guess I should point out, just in the interest of fairness) said that Sam's threats against me and his putting his hands on me did constitute an assault, even if his assault against me didn't send me to the sports medicine clinic for an MRI that turned up nothing wrong.

I guess the courts don't really want to deal with pissant crimi-nals like Sam and me, so they appointed this mediator.

Neither Sam nor I said much, but our dads were both doing that extra-polite-just-to-let-you-know-I-really-want-to-choke-the-shit-out-of-you thing with each other. I actually thought it was kind of ballsy of Dad, who, as we've seen, is a pussified Hallmark card at least half the time.

In the end, I got sixteen hours of community service to Sam's eight, and we both got probation for six months. "Get caught at a kegger, get caught with so much as a marijuana seed in your pos-session, and you're going to juvenile lockup for thirty days," the mediator said.

This was not much of a punishment for me, but Sam looked daggers at me. The MRI had shown that his college scholarship might be intact, but six months without keggers is social death at our school. Ha.

What did you ever see in this guy? I texted to Neilly.

A minute later, this came back: *H. O. T. T.* I had no response to that.

After I got home, I texted this to Chantelle: *Got probation. Sorry.* No response. *I mean, that's not normally something I do.* Nothing. *Kicking the guy, I mean.* The same thing. *Do you hate me?*

She didn't answer this one, either, but I assumed she was

following the antistalker protocol of cutting off all contact.

I asked Neilly for help, and she did manage to talk to Chantelle, who wouldn't so much as meet my eyes at school.

"So?" I asked Neilly in the hall by her locker after lunch, when I had seen her talking to Chantelle.

"Uh, so move on. You blew this one."

"And here I was hoping she'd blow me."

"If I didn't know that your disgusting exterior hides a kind of sweet kid, I don't think I'd ever talk to you again, much less do you a huge favor like have an incredibly awkward conversation with a girl who hates you." Sweet. *Nice* is the kiss of death, but *sweet* is okay. Hmm.

"Did she say that?"

"Didn't have to, but her meaning was crystal clear. That is a total dead end. Lots of fish in the sea, et cetera. Move on."

Or, perhaps, move in? I mean, there was one girl here who doesn't hate me. Well, actually two.

"Okay, what about Lulu? I mean, is that a possibility?"

"She said I'm really lucky to have such a cool brother."

"Yeah?"

"And she hoped you'd think of her as a sister, too."

"Sister?! Out of the boyfriend pool! Crap!"

"Don't you have all kinds of metal babes you know from the scene? I thought there were piercings involved."

"Nondrinking, nonsmoking metal fans not currently attached

to gigantic guys with Satan tattooed on their colossal biceps? Negative. I made that shit up."

"I knew that. All right. This is a problem we can solve. But in the meantime, I'm gonna be late for chemistry."

The more I thought about it, the clearer the solution seemed. Not sure it was clear to everyone involved, though. Neilly ran off down the hall, and I slipped into study hall before the proctor even got there.

I, by which I mean Dad, decided to get my community service out of the way as soon as possible, so I was scheduled to meet my fellow convicts at six a.m. outside of the county jail—no, really, it sounds like something out of a country song or something, but it really was the county jail, or, to be more precise, the Edwin Meese Justice Center of Burr County. There we would take a bus to Paine Park, an eighty-five-acre park that, it turns out, is maintained entirely by "volunteer" labor. I think it's stretching it to call my service "volunteering," since my other option was thirty days in juvenile lockup, but whatever.

Dad seemed to take great pleasure out of waking me up at five thirty on a Saturday morning. "Coffee," I murmured, and that was the only word I spoke to the old man until he dropped me off and I stood clutching a paper cup of coffee with Immortal's "Antarctica" pummeling my eardrums through my headphones, at five fifty a.m. at the Edwin Meese Justice Center.

"See you at two!" Dad said, chipper. I tried not to think about what he and Neilly's mom might get up to in a house that would be empty for eight hours.

I know this is probably kind of racist—okay, no, scratch that, it's totally racist—but I kind of expected to be sitting on a bus with a bunch of black and Hispanic bandanna-sporting gang bangers like they have on TV. Okay, so I'm a dumb, sheltered white kid. So dumb, in fact, that I didn't realize that apart from Chantelle and her dad, and Emerson at church—who was on the beach at Normandy on D-Day and is the coolest old guy ever— there really aren't any black people in Burr County, and the only Hispanic person anyone's ever seen owns Lupita's Mexican Restaurant and would be unlikely to be doing litter duty with a bunch of juvenile offenders.

No, I was surrounded by a bunch of stringy-haired, addicted-to-God-knows-what, unwashed white kids. I immediately gravitated to the rather colossal kid with the full beard who was wearing a Behemoth shirt. He looked at my own Dimmu Borgir shirt and nodded approval. We bumped fists, and I felt somewhat okay about this whole adventure—for one thing, I was already cool with the biggest kid here, so my odds of ending the day with all my limbs still attached had just increased dramatically. But for another thing, I got immediately that what went on here was like the Bizarro World version of school—the weirder and angrier you looked, the more you were accepted.

What would be tough in this crowd would be being a regular normal popular kid.

And speaking of which, Sam rolled up in his SUV—which did not have a vanity plate that read IMATOOL, but might as well have—and hopped out. He was dressed head to toe in Abercrombie, and though he was not wearing a big target on his head, everyone could see one there anyway. He took one look at this crowd and looked like he might soil himself. Yeah, his eight hours were going to be a lot tougher than my sixteen.

I turned back to the guy in the Behemoth shirt. "So what are you in for?" he said. I was glad he had asked first, because I was afraid to ask him.

"Assault," I said, and he gave me a respectful nod.

"Possession," he said. "I was holding one point one ounces, and you know what the dumb thing is? I don't even smoke. It puts me to sleep. I was honest to God holding it for a friend. But you can't tell the cops something like that. You might get your mom to believe it, but the cops don't care."

"Yeah, I guess not."

"You in a band?"

"Nah. You?"

"I play guitar for Slaughter of the Innocents. We've only played a few shows, but we're getting better. You should check out our Facebook page."

"I totally will."

It was a genial bus ride from then on, with me and my new friend, whose real name was Ulf Lovhammer. How badass is that? His parents are actual Swedes, and his last name is Lovhammer. Awesome.

Okay, I was kind of following Ulf around in a semi-embarrassing fanboy daze, so it took me a while to realize that Sam was getting hazed by the freaks and degenerates in the back of the bus, like—well, like the freaks and degenerates got hazed by guys like him at school.

"Hey, Tom Brady, you're kinda pretty," they said.

"Tom Brady, you get probation for your football team sucking ass last week?"

Stuff like this. Dumb and mean.

We arrived at the park, and hours and hours of boredom followed as we picked up beer can after beer can, as well as the occasional syringe and crack pipe. Yeah, the park is a classy place. Sam was the lucky lottery winner who stabbed a used condom with his pointy stick, and as he was putting it into his garbage bag, he got, "Oh, my fault, Tom Brady! I left that behind when I was up here with your mom last night!"

Sam turned red and said nothing.

Meanwhile, Ulf told me how Slaughter of the Innocents was a vegan black metal band, and that one of the reasons they started is that they wanted to educate people about animal suffering, but mostly he wanted to prove to people that vegans aren't pussies.

"People think we're a bunch of sandal-wearing hippies, and then we get onstage and shred their faces off; it's kinda cool."

Meanwhile, the troglodytes taunting Sam were actually starting to annoy me. "Tom Brady," they said over and over again, and I kind of started to feel bad for old Jocky. I mean, at school, I get to escape from the taunts of guys like Sam—to be totally fair, I've never actually heard Sam call me Columbine or otherwise say anything abusive, but I've definitely seen him stand there while his buddies did. But here in Paine Park, there was nowhere Sam could run to get away from the jeers of idiots. I guess this shows that I did inherit some of my dad's sentimentality or something, but I just started thinking, *What if I was stuck doing something like this with Sam and all his friends? How bad would it suck to have them riding me all day long? And if Sam insisted at the end that he'd heard everything but never actually done anything to stop it, would I still think he was a piece of shit?*

"Hey, morons, will you get a new taunt?" I finally yelled at the dumb hyenas. "That 'Tom Brady' shit is getting really old."

The hyenas were not too physically imposing, but there were three of them. They turned on me. "You gay for Tom Brady?"

I hate this crap. I don't know if it's just from having grown up with Sarah and Lisa or what, but it pisses me off when guys like these say "gay" like it's the worst thing in the world. "Yeah. As a matter of fact, I am. And we're both in here because I caught him with another guy, and we beat the crap out of each other. So yeah, I'm, like, a little pissed at him right now, but seriously, leave my boyfriend alone."

The hyenas didn't know how to respond—the script called for me to defend my heterosexuality and thereby provoke a fight, but it took them a minute to process what I'd said, and they had no response. Except to start moving toward me. And me without my steel-toed shoes.

"You guys don't want to do that," Ulf said in his best vegan black metal growl. They looked up at him and decided that maybe they actually didn't want to do that.

"Fags," they said over their shoulders as they took their pointy sticks and trash bags to another part of the park.

I said "Thanks" to Ulf just as Sam was saying it to me. My jaw dropped nearly to the ground.

"It's nothing," Ulf said.

I turned to Sam and said, "No problem. But I hope you know this means we are totally going to prom together now."

Sam looked at my face, saw that I was joking, and actually laughed.

CHAPTER TWELVE

Neilly

MY DAD CALLED IN HIS FAVOR AT THE WORST POSSIBLE moment. I'd just heard a rumor that Sam had hooked up with Suzy Melendez over the weekend, I'd gotten a D on a pop quiz in trig, and I'd tripped with a full food tray in front of the entire cafeteria. So suffice to say, I was already in a pretty bad mood. But when my dad came to pick me up for our regularly scheduled Wednesday night dinner and sprang it on me that Roger and Griffin would be joining us, it got even worse.

"Daaaa-ad," I whined. "Can't it just be me and you tonight? I don't feel like playing nice with anyone else."

My dad gave me a stern look. It kind of scorched my soul a little, because my dad normally looks at me like I'm a rare and unique creature he can't quite believe exists. "Neilly, I did you a big favor the other day, getting Declan out of trouble. Now it's time to return that favor."

I knew he was right, but I couldn't quite let it go at that, so I went for the jugular: massive guilt. "Don't you think I've had enough new 'family' members thrown at me lately?"

I put my fingers up in air quotes and made a face when I said *family*—because family was mom and me, dad and me, and/or the three of us together. Not this jumble of random people I wasn't related to and hadn't chosen to have in my life. They were only there because of who my parents were sleeping with, and that seemed like a pretty dumb reason for me to have to befriend someone.

"I'm not trying to force a new family down your throat, Neilly. But Roger and I are just as legitimate a couple as your mom and Thomas are. And that means, like it or not, our families are going to have to blend sometimes. Not only on holidays and special occasions but also for everyday things like our Wednesday night dinners."

"But I don't *want* to blend," I yelled at him so loudly I surprised even myself. "I hate this goddamn blender you and mom put me in, and I want to get the fuck out of it. Now!"

"Don't use the F-bomb around me, Neilly," my dad said in a quiet voice that probably didn't begin to convey how upset he was with me. "And I really don't appreciate the lack of respect you're showing for what's important to me."

I crossed my arms over my chest and said nothing. I mean, there was nothing to say, right? I had zero say about anything that happened to me anymore, and that was that.

My dad gripped the steering wheel so hard his knuckles went albino. "Would this be any different if Roger was named, say, Rachel? Is that what this is about?"

"No!" I yelled even louder now. "God, how can you even *ask* me that? After all I've gone through at school? After every fight I've gotten into because I was sticking up for your right to choose who to love, even if it's a guy? I think I've gone above and beyond the call of duty, dude."

"Okay, okay," he said, putting his blinker on and turning into the parking lot of a fancy French restaurant.

That pissed me off even more. Our usual dinner out consists of going to my favorite place—Meatheads—where I always get the same large basket of cheese fries with buffalo ranch dipping sauce. And I totally wasn't in the mood for freaking snails or duck liver or whatever gross stuff they served at this joint.

"I appreciate your being open-minded and loyal, Neilly. I really do," Dad said. "But I don't think I should have to apologize for who I am for the rest of my life."

I sighed heavily. "You don't ever have to apologize for that, Dad," I told him. "Just like I shouldn't have to apologize for not wanting to get all buddy-buddy with someone I'd never choose to be friends with under any other circumstances."

My dad cut the engine. "Maybe you could practice some of that open-mindedness on Griffin, honey. You've never even met him."

"And if I had my way, I never would," I mumbled. If my dad heard me, he ignored it.

"It's not like I'm asking you to fall in love with him, Neilly— just be friendly, okay? Or, at the very least, cordial."

Even though Dad had roped me into a dumb getting-to-know-you dinner, I still wasn't buying into the friendly or cordial part. I trudged into the restaurant behind my dad, dragging my feet, with my eyes on the ground and a huge scowl on my face.

And when I finally looked up, there was Roger. With my hottie from youth group standing right next to him. Disappointment doesn't begin to describe what I was feeling at that moment. Figures I'd only be attracted to the dickiest guy on Earth. Why couldn't I just go for nice guys? The ones who actually chose *not* to cheat when tempted, the ones who didn't dump their dad because of his sexual preferences?

Griffin smiled at me warmly. I gave him the cold shoulder.

"Hey, Neilly, nice to finally meet you," he said. "I've seen you at youth group, right?"

I nodded, my brain trying to figure out how my body could be so attracted to someone so wrong for me. For a merit scholar, sometimes I was the biggest dumbass on the planet.

Meanwhile, my dad put a hand on Griffin's shoulder. "Can you keep Neilly company for a few minutes while your dad and I go iron out a few last-minute details about our reception?"

"Sure," he said. "This is a great place to have a wedding party. And my dad tells me the band's going to be totally smokin'."

"Smoking is right . . . ," I mumbled as my dad and Roger walked away.

"Excuse me?" Griffin asked politely.

I shrugged. "Your eyes. They're red as tomatoes."

"What's that supposed to mean?"

I ignored him, feeling black and mean and void inside.

"No, tell me."

I pointed to my eyes, then his. It was like I was doing a bad imitation of the father in *Meet the Parents*. Griffin took out a small bottle from his pocket and squeezed some drops into his eyes. "Thanks for reminding me."

"Yeah, you wouldn't want your dad to realize you're all wasted, huh?"

"Is that what you think I am?"

I shrugged again.

Griffin cocked his head and gave me a long look. "So what else do you think you know about me?"

I started in on him without even thinking. "For starters, how you have to stay after school practically every day. You run with a crowd that'll be lucky to get a job at a gas station after graduation. And that you totally ditch out on people any time you feel like it, no matter who it hurts. I mean, you can't even go to youth group without bailing early!"

Griffin just sat there and took it. I figured his lack of response meant he had nothing to say—because everything I'd said was all true. And if the truth hurt, tough shit. He'd made his bed; now he could lie in it.

"Well, you're right about one thing. I'm not perfect," he finally said.

"That's an understatement." How dare Griffin ice his father like that and lay judgment on mine in the process? I didn't care that he'd decided to speak to his dad again. It didn't change what he'd done, or the pain he'd caused.

Griffin pulled the bottle of what I'd assumed was Visine out of his pocket and handed it to me. I glanced down at the label. It read: *Vigamox.*

"So?"

"So I got pink eye after the last youth group. The doctor thought it was probably from the blindfolds."

That explained his beet-red eyes. A tinge of guilt washed through my belly. Then I thought: *So he's not stoned now. Big deal. He'll probably go to his bedroom and toke it up once he gets home.* "Bummer."

"And as for staying after school every day and hanging with

a group of so-called losers," he went on. "I teach English as a second language to kids whose parents come here from other countries looking for a better life. I also fill in for the teacher of the Sunday night classes, and that's why I have to leave youth group early sometimes. So yeah, those kids would be thrilled to graduate and get a job at the gas station so they could send money back home to their relatives who are living in conditions you and I can't even imagine."

"Good for you." Fine, so he was trying to make up for the shitty way he'd treated his own family by helping people he wasn't related to. All that proved was that he wasn't 100 percent bad. I still wasn't ready to be all, like, *Ooh, I was wrong about you, aren't you fabulous!*

Griffin sighed. "And as for ditching people who love me . . . Neilly, maybe your mom was fine with everything that went down, but mine wasn't. In fact, when it all hit, she didn't even get out of bed for a month. Do you have any idea what it's like going to school wondering if your mother is going to off herself while you're gone? Or having to feed her like a baby, because if you don't she won't eat? What about having to figure out how the hell to do all the laundry because there are no clean clothes left to wear in the house?"

I shook my head, feeling as low as a cockroach. My mom had pretty much taken the news in stride, telling me she and my dad would always love each other but hadn't been "in love" for a long, long time. They were more like best friends than anything, and they had remained so even after Roger entered the picture. So no, it wasn't like the divorce had anywhere near as much impact on my life as it apparently had had on Griffin's.

"When you see someone you love in pain like that, it makes you want to lash out at the thing that hurt them," he went on. "And that thing was my dad. I couldn't believe he'd done that to my mom, and so yeah, I went radio silence on him. I regret it now, but at the time, I thought maybe it would make him come back. And that maybe if he came back, she'd get better."

I nodded. I could only imagine what I might've done under the same circumstances. "So it wasn't about you being ashamed of your dad because he's gay?"

"Nope."

"So I was wrong about you this whole time?" I whispered.

He answered my question with a question. "Do you always believe everything you hear without finding out the truth for yourself first?"

"No," I said, even as it hit me that the answer was really yes. I had my defenses up so high, I automatically assumed the worst from everyone, even my best friend. Like, I thought if I never put my total faith in someone, it would shield me from getting hurt. How wrong I'd been. "Well, maybe."

Griffin wrapped up the whole messy conversation with milder words than I deserved. "So now you know all about my sordid ways, and I know all about yours."

"I guess we do," I said, tacking on a quiet little "Sorry" at the end.

"Forgiven," he said, his whole face softening. "You know, I have this theory: without forgiveness, we'd all be walking this Earth angry and alone, and I think that would really suck. Don't you?"

My eyes flew open and I sucked in my breath. So Roger's son—the guy I'd held a grudge against for so long—was actually my mental *and* physical crush from youth group, all wrapped up in one person? How was that possible? Weren't the odds of that happening, like, less than zero?

"I think I've actually heard that one before," I said, a little smile playing on my lips. I only hoped he could apply his forgiveness theory to me. "And I have to admit, up until you said that, I had no clue you were my partner in all those games at youth group. Did you know it was me this whole time?"

"I was pretty sure once you started giving me a hard time," he said with a laugh. "You've got this really sweet little voice. Such a small voice for such a big personality."

"Well, I really like that forgiveness thing you told me about," I said, feeling suddenly shy and exposed. "I even used it in my life, and it totally worked. My best friend and I made up, and I have you to thank for it."

"That's awesome!" he said. "But let me tell you a secret. That whole theory's not just about my forgiving other people. It's also about believing I deserved to *be* forgiven, you know?"

I thought about that one for a second, then said, "I get that. And I think you're all cool there. Roger seems thrilled to have you back in his life. I mean, he talks about you all the time."

Roger and my dad reappeared from their last-minute wedding planning before we could discuss it any further—but we'd already said enough to smooth everything over on this side of the blended family. So we went and had a not just cordial but downright friendly dinner. Only my dad ordered snails, and I even learned something: pommes frites are these awesomely crispy french fries, and they're almost as good as the ones at Meatheads.

I apologized to my dad on the drive home for being so stubborn and mean, and he accepted. After such a bad beginning to the day, I ended up feeling a lot better than I had in a really long time. Which is why what happened next freaked me out so much. My dad and I had settled into a comfortable silence in the car, and I was busy thinking about everything Griffin and I had talked about and how different he was from all the other guys I knew, when I got a text.

From Sam.

Consisting of just three words:

Don't hate me.

Followed by a killer three more:

I miss u.

CHAPTER THIRTEEN

DECLAN

MY COMMUNITY SERVICE ASSIGNMENTS WERE TWO Saturdays apart because (a) I work on Sundays, and (b) oh yeah, we had to leave the only home I'd ever known on the Saturday in between.

Dad went into hyper-efficiency mode, totally focused on all the details. I had minimal possessions, so I could pack up my entire life in pretty much one evening, which left me way too much time to think.

I didn't like what I was thinking about—like my Neilly problem. I mean, at first, I just lusted after her like pretty much any other heterosexual guy in school might. But now I appeared to be developing an actual crush on her. It's just that I talked to her more than I talked to any other girl, and I liked her a lot. And she knew who I really was, and she seemed to like me anyway. And though this kind of thing makes girls cross guys off the boyfriend list, for me it's incredibly hot.

But, of course, I'd gone from off her radar to completely taboo, and she was hot for Griffin anyway, even if she didn't realize it yet, and, oh yeah, my ex-boyfriend Sam was chasing her again, too. So who wants a scrawny guy you're sort of related to when you can have either Jocky McMoron or Shaggy McDanger? I needed to think about something else.

Except that the other thing I was thinking about was Mom, what with us actually getting ready to move and everything.

So I tried to think about other stuff. I checked out Slaughter of the Innocents's Facebook page, their demos fed my guts through a wood chipper and had me begging for more, and so I sent Ulf Lovhammer a message just saying, like, *Hey, remember me from community service, your band rocks my socks off, when are you playing next*—stuff like that.

He sent me twenty-one tracks of devastation and a bunch of links to animal rights websites, vegan information, and other stuff. And because my alternatives were thinking about Neilly or thinking about Mom or having Dad order me to do something heinous like Bubble Wrap the champagne flutes, I spent a lot of time on the vegan websites.

And though listening to Satanic metal had never inspired me

orship Satan (the whole thing always just seemed like a goof to me—a red guy with horns and a tail. Like, why not worship Freddy Krueger or something?), the vegan metal had me thinking seriously about going vegan. I mean, I have to confess, I thought vegans were all wussy, hairy stoners, but really, refusing to eat animal products seems like such a total rejection of normal society that it's actually badass.

That's what I tried to tell myself anyway. The truth is actually somewhat less macho: the factory farm videos kind of did me in. The chicken stuff was enough to put me off the Kung Pao, but the footage of pig farms actually made me start crying. For, like, a half hour, I just sat there with my head in my hands—how the hell did I not know this? I just felt so bad for those pigs, raised in jail and tortured until they die, that the idea of frying them up and eating them with breakfast made me want to cry all over again.

I showed Dad, and he said, "Yeah, Dec, that's horrifying stuff. But can we do one massive life change at a time, please?"

The hell with that. He sprang a bunch on me, so I figured it was my turn to spring one on him. I knew Dr. Gordon might ask me if the suffering I was sad about was really a nine-year-old kid with a dead mom and not a baby pig. I don't care about the answer to that question. If ordering from the veggie section of the Chinese menu makes me feel like I'm helping either one of them, that's cool with me.

We continued to tear our old life apart, but it was nice for me to have something else to think about.

So I was pretty immersed in learning everything I could about being a vegan until Friday night, also known as Dad-loses-his-shit night. I sat in my room calmly looking at videos shot without permission by activists breaking and entering at factory farms (How badass is that? No Satanic metalhead has ever done something that cool.) when Dad came storming in.

"Dec! Jesus! Will you get up and help me, please?" he bellowed.

"Dad, could you knock? I could have been engaged in the act of self-love in here, and that's not something you—"

"No time to even be disgusted. I'm screwed. I started packing the attic up the other night and totally forgot to finish. Take these"—he thrust some cardboard boxes, a marker, and a packing-tape dispenser at me—"and go make sure every box in the attic is sealed and ready to go, and everything not in a box gets boxed up. And label it all. Thank you. Movers arrive at seven a.m. tomorrow. Looks like I'm pulling an all-nighter in the garage."

And just like that he was gone, and I was holding moving supplies. Well, I guess the farm videos could wait. I headed up to the attic and found that Dad, mercifully, had been freaking out about nothing. There were maybe ten open boxes up here, plus a couple of piles of stuff that would fit into about three other boxes, in my estimation. I threw all the loose crap into boxes, sealed them up, and wrote *Attic* on them within about five minutes.

And then I started sealing up the other boxes, and one of the open ones said, *P—H.S. P* being my mom's first initial. And yeah, her name was actually Patience because her parents were big Gilbert and Sullivan fans, and I give her a lot of credit for never killing them in their sleep for that.

And *H.S.*, I assumed, stood for *high school*.

Not wanting to mess myself up by thinking about Mom, I wisely sealed up the box, stuck it next to the others, and never so much as glanced at the contents.

At least, this is what I told myself I should do. What I actually did was tear into it like I was starving and it was full of cruelty-free food. I mean, I guess I really was starving, because while I'd certainly gotten my fill of learning about Dad in a way that's more than the way little kids know their parents, I didn't know squat about Mom except that she was my mom.

And here was a box of clues to her identity.

Some random snapshots. Mom, her hair incredibly short, sporting jeans, low-top Converse, and a white T-shirt with STRAIGHT EDGE written on it in black. Mom, hair still incredibly short, dressed in a red-and-green sweater and a preppy kilt and standing next to Aunt Josephine. The trained eye can see that Mom's kilt is fastened not with the same kind of gigantic safety pin that holds Aunt Josephine's kilt together, but rather with a tiny pin that reads MINOR THREAT.

Mom was so badass that Grandma demanded she wear that nice preppy outfit she'd bought for the Christmas card picture, and Mom couldn't do it, couldn't be normal for even one photograph—she had to have the Minor Threat pin there. Oh my God, I loved my mom so much it hurt. Which must be why I was crying.

Dammit, Mom, where the hell are you? I need you.

She wasn't there, of course. Just the pictures, a couple of yearbooks (Mom had short hair when every other girl in the entire school had hair the size of New Jersey—because she was the coolest), and some of her punk rock paraphernalia, including the Minor Threat badge from the photo, which I quickly affixed to my Slaughter of the Innocents T-shirt and vowed to wear every day.

And what looked like a math notebook, but which turned out to be some kind of journal. The dead have no privacy to invade, so I dove right in.

Senior year. Big fucking deal. Mom! Such a potty mouth! *Last night I asked Mom if she thought Dad would have stopped drinking if they'd named me Temperance instead of Patience, ha-ha. Mom screamed at me. Dad's just got an upset stomach, he gets an ulcer from the stress of work, you don't know what the hell you're talking about.*

Yeah, well, I know who's a drunk in this house. And I know who loves booze more than me. And I know who loves the drunk who loves booze more than me more than me. Can't wait to get out—out of horrible DHS, out of Massachusetts, out of the sickness and the lies and everything that makes me hate it here.

Oh, Mom, I thought, I don't know what it's like to grow up with a drunk for a dad, but I get the anger. Loud and clear. I flip through.

The 'Mats totally sold out, Stink was their last good record, so why did I go? (Tommy Stinson, duh.) I was just trying to enjoy the old stuff, yelling out for "Fuck School," stuff like that, and who comes up to me but Thomas from school. Hey, that, unless I miss my guess, is my dad! *In a freaking Smiths shirt.* Yep, that's Dad all right. *He was all trying to talk to me, and I was like, "I'm not talking to you with that beer in your hand, loser."* Dad with the underage drinking! And the Smiths shirt! What a tool! *So he threw the beer at Paul Westerberg, and they nearly stopped the show he was so pissed, and I guess he thought he was being funny, but it was just such a loser move, like I'm going to be impressed that he threw a beer at the stage. Loser, loser, loser.*

I felt I had to stick up for Dad here. That was a pretty badass move, considering it could have gotten him arrested and/or beaten senseless, and he did it to impress a girl. That's gotta count for something!

Apparently not, or at least not at first. A couple of months go by until Dad's name comes up again.

Thomas came up to me out of nowhere, like I know him only from English class and when he stopped the 'Mats from playing "Gary's Got a Boner" in the middle, which actually wasn't that bad of a move, and he was like, "Listen, I don't know if you have prom plans, but I've got Elvis Costello tickets for prom night, and I'd much rather go see Elvis Costello with you than go to some lameass dance."

I told him I would think about it, which I am now doing. I don't like Elvis Costello, but I guess I like him more than prom—stupid ritual with stupid . . . ah, but I was kind of looking forward to being all girly. I guess that would blow my image, but there you go. I kind of wanted to get all dressed up. I snagged that awesome vintage gown at the thrift store. Plus, I don't really get why Thomas asked me. I mean,

aren't there, like, some New Wave chicks he could ask or something?
Elvis Costello, or awesome vintage dress and hearing horrible music
until I can't stand it anymore and then ditching the stupid after par-
ties because everyone will be drinking, and if I want that shit, I'd just
as soon come home where at least I can lock myself in my room.

I guess I knew how this came out, because here I am, and
named after Elvis Costello, too, but I kept reading anyway. And
found, to my horror, my badass mom totally wussified by the
power of love. Here's all she had to say the day after the concert.

So yeah, we went to Elvis Costello in our prom clothes, which was
Thomas's idea, and he is really sweet, and I really like him, and
I guess I like Elvis Costello now, and yeah even a guy who walks
around wearing Smiths shirts who turns out to be an amazing kisser.

Which is where I bailed, because if she got into any more
detail about their late-night activities together, I may have had
to vomit copiously.

I closed the journal, but I didn't put it in the box.

I headed out to the garage. Dad was in a boxing-and-sealing
frenzy. "Dad," I called out. "Attic's done."

He raised his head. "Thanks, Dec. You rock."

"No, Dad, you rock. You threw beer on Paul Westerberg!"

He stopped, looked at me, and took in the Minor Threat pin and
the journal. "Is that what she said? It was actually Bob Stinson, and
he was so shitfaced he didn't even notice. Do you know I've never
even read that?"

"Do you want to?"

"Nah. If she'd wanted me to read it, she would have shown me when she was alive. It's between you and her now."

Something occurred to me. "Did you want me to find this?"

"Duh, Dec. There are like five boxes in the attic. I could have done that myself. Yeah, I wanted you to find it. I wanted you to know that just because we're leaving this house doesn't mean we're leaving her. We can't leave her. She's in our hearts, you know? So we can't leave her."

I was pissed. Pissed about his crafty little scheme, and also because he was going all Hallmark-y on me again and trying to get me to cry. So I changed the subject.

"So Dad, where'd you get the stones to pursue a badass like Mom, anyway?"

Dad just smiled. "Born with 'em, son. Born with 'em."

Well. The next day I was moving in with Neilly Foster, also kind of a badass in her own gorgeous-popular-girl way. And yeah, it would be weird, and awkward, and all that stuff, but I didn't care. She wasn't my real sister, and she wouldn't even be my stepsister until they got married. She'd just be some incredibly hot girl who thinks I'm sweet and who laughs at my jokes and who happens to live down the hall. Hell, if that scenario was taboo, nobody would ever get laid at college.

Yep. If Dad could go after what he wanted, then dammit, so could I.

CHAPTER FOURTEEN

Neilly

I WAS STILL THINKING ABOUT SAM'S TEXT A FEW DAYS later. I hadn't done anything about it, but it hadn't left my mind, either.

Don't hate me. I miss u.

Now what was that supposed to mean?

I mean, I knew what it meant. Sam didn't want me to hate him. Plus, he missed me. Maybe he missed how we used to meet for mochas on Saturday mornings. Or how we'd always text each other *make a wish* before going to sleep at night. Or the way I used to trace my finger around his biceps.

I was mulling over all the possibilities when I realized *why* wasn't what really mattered. Whether I'd even be willing to give him a chance to explain it was. And if I did, where would that leave my complicated feelings for Griffin?

I was still debating that one in my mind when my mom pulled up a seat beside me. Her red bandanna tied as a doo-rag and baggy sweatpants made her look so unintentionally ghetto I had to laugh.

"It's nice to see you smiling for once," she said.

"You hoping to become a rapper in your next life?" I asked, instead of getting on her case for the annoying comment. I was just so tired of fighting with everyone.

"Yo yo yo!" my mom started freestyling badly. "I'm just a pregnant mama, who loves her only daughta, but she's saying that I oughta get blown out of the water, for leading her to the slaughterhouse tomorra, it's such a horror . . ."

I gave her a little smattering of applause. At least she was trying.

"Don't quit my day job, huh?" she asked, grabbing the bandanna from her head and tossing it on the table. She looked completely spent, probably a result of trying to pack up our entire lives these past few weeks.

"Definitely not."

"I might, you know, once this little one is born," she said, patting her ever-increasing pregnancy bump. "I think being a mom to two teenagers and one infant will be a big enough job without complicating matters by having to work forty-plus hours a week."

"Mom, no offense, but you shouldn't start thinking you're

Dec's mom just because you and his dad are together," I told her. "He's really sensitive about that stuff, and besides, it's not true. You're going to be his sort-of stepmom at best. I mean, the guy's sixteen already. He's way too old to have someone new in his life trying to parent him."

She sighed. "I know. It's just that my heart goes out to that kid. I feel like he really needs a mother figure in his life, especially at his age, with all the girl questions he must have."

I couldn't help but think maybe she was right. Dec's date with Chantelle—which, despite all my coaching, had turned into a complete and utter disaster—was the first and last time I'd ever known him to hang out with a girl other than me. And now that poor girl was terrified of him, skittering out of the room anytime she even caught a glimpse of the guy. The truly sad part was, beneath his sharp metal exterior, Dec was a total softie. I'd been trying to think of a way to help him back into Chantelle's good graces, but so far I'd found myself SOL.

"So now you're an expert on dating?"

"Well, I've definitely learned a thing or two over the years," she said. "And I'd love to share what I know with Dec. Even with you, if you'd listen."

"Thanks, but I've already got full-blown gaydar, Mom," I told her. "I think yours might've been a little on the fritz the first time around."

I expected her to get all pissed and to yell at me like she has so often lately—most of the times, I'll admit, I deserved it—but instead she threw her head back and started laughing. "You know, when I met your father, androgyny was huge. Guy-liner, glam, the works. I mean, even the football players looked more stereotypically gay than your dad, so how was I supposed to know?"

I tried to imagine my father all Flock of Seagulls, or whatever lame bands they used to love, but just could not get there. He was so . . . well, plain old dad-ish now. Slightly balding, a little paunch under the shirt, graying at the temples. "Maybe by the way he checked out other guys in bars instead of girls?"

"It was never like that," my mom said, still laughing a little. This was the most civil—hell, even enjoyable—conversation we'd had since the shit hit the fan. She shook her head. "Have you ever wondered how you could be so wrong about someone?"

I thought of Dec and Lu, then Griffin. "Yeah," I said. "I actually have."

"Much as I love the fact that you're actually speaking to me, Neilly, we should be getting to bed," she said, patting my hand. "Big day tomorrow."

I glanced at the clock and laughed. "Mom, it's only nine thirty."

"Okay, let me rephrase that. *I* should be going to bed. This pregnancy thing is exhausting at my age."

"Night then," I said.

She stood up and put her mug in the sink. "So, do you still hate me over all this?"

I looked up at her, startled. "All of what?"

"New baby, stepfather, house. I really threw you some curve-balls, didn't I?"

"I don't hate you, Mom," I told her. "I never did. I never could."

"I love you, too, baby," she said, echoing the words I hadn't said but totally meant.

After video chatting with Lu practically all night—damn, it felt good to have her back in my life—I was not in the best shape to move. Yet there it was, moving day, and so I had to move my butt out of bed and into a car loaded to the roof with stuff my mom and I had accumulated over a lifetime, and then move those zillions of accumulated articles into the House of Horrors.

As I brought the first box over the threshold and looked around, I gasped. Even I had to admit Dec and his dad had done an absolutely amazing job renovating the place. I'd paid attention to the progress on my room and my room only over the past few weeks—I figured if I had a safe haven in this horror show, everything would be kind of okay-ish—but now it was like everything had changed. Who would've thought two scrawny guys like Dec and his dad could transform this hell house into a cool as hell house, especially so quickly. I mean, the place was still creepy, but in a very MTV *Cribs* kind of way. My friends were gonna freak over it.

I was still staring around in awe when Dec came shuffling into the foyer with a steaming hot mug of what looked like solid black mud. "Want some?"

"Not unless you can make me a grande skinny vanilla latte," I said with a smirk. Dec hates girly coffee drinks.

"Coming right up!" Dec's father piped in from the kitchen.

"He's kidding, right?"

Dec shook his head, his eyes blacker than his coffee. "Unfortunately, no. Dad has broken the man code and gone and bought a fancy espresso machine for the chicks in the house."

"That's so cool!"

"No, it's not."

"Oh yes, it is!"

A minute later, Dec's dad appeared with the most perfect latte in the world. Foam white as snow topped off the beautiful, creamy, caramel-colored liquid. I took a sip. Way better than Starbucks. "I'm beginning to think I might not totally hate living here."

"I'm glad to hear that, Neilly," he said. "Your mom and I have been pretty worried about how hard you two took the news. . . ."

Dec and I shared a look and a nod.

"I think we're cool now," I said, almost believing it.

"Maybe," Dec added.

"So you know what I think we should do to celebrate maybe not hating it here once we get settled in?" I didn't even wait for an answer. "Have the most kickass Halloween party ever."

The dark clouds broke up, and Dec actually smiled. With his teeth showing and everything. "Now you're talkin'. Maybe my friend Ulf's band could even play!"

"Well then, kids," Dec's dad said. "Let's get moving. Halloween is just around the corner."

By the time Monday night rolled around, I was still totally exhausted from hauling and unpacking all those boxes. Youth group was the last place I was interested in going. Really, my bed was the only thing calling my name.

But Dec insisted. "I cannot watch those two play goo-goo eyes for another second this week," he said, referring to our very-much-visibly-in-love parents. "You gotta get me out of here for at least a couple of hours."

And so I dragged my butt into the shower, got dressed, dried my hair, and went for a totally-adorable-without-trying-too-hard kind of look. Downstairs, Dec was waiting for me.

Giving me the most bewildered look ever.

"What?" I asked.

"Nothing."

"Then why are you looking at me like that?"

"I guess I'm still getting used to the fact that we're living together now," he told me.

"Ooo-kay," I said. "Let's not make this weirder than it already is. We are going to youth group now, and I'm driving, since your permit doesn't allow you out after dark unless a parent is in the car with you. Got it?"

"Got it."

Once we got there, I realized I probably should've just stayed at home. Nothing Aunt Sarah was saying about our unique gifts and talents, trusting in them, and not keeping them a secret from the world was sinking in. It was all just a big huge blahblahblah, no offense to Aunt Sarah.

Plus, Griffin wasn't anywhere to be found, and even though that should've made it easier for me to concentrate, it just made it harder. I couldn't help wondering if he was off teaching ESL again or just plain old avoiding me. And then when he finally *did* slide into the packed room five minutes late and smiled at me, I couldn't stop obsessing over whether it had been a friendly smile or just a cordial one.

The first sentence Aunt Sarah said that actually registered with me was this: "So, here's a surprise. I'm not going to be blindfolding you guys in pairs this time."

I should have been relieved—that meant no awkward one-on-one time with Griffin. But instead, I found myself kind of disappointed. Because I guess I'd kind of been looking forward to some awkward one-on-one time with him.

Then Aunt Sarah added, "Tonight you're actually going to meet the person you've been partnered up with over the past few weeks. And you're going to take a big leap of faith, trusting him or her with your thoughts face-to-face. The topic is this: your proudest moment and your biggest regret, and how these relate to the special gifts given to you by your Higher Power."

Now she was talkin'.

"Sooooooo," Griffin said once we'd sat down.

"Sooooooo."

"We meet again."

"That we do." I was totally grinning at him by this point.

"Want me to start?" he asked, matching my smile with an even bigger one of his own.

While that would've been easier, I was slowly gathering my Nerves of Steely Neilly to be used in a kinder, gentler manner than I usually do. "No, let me," I said, getting serious. "My biggest regret, at least lately, is being so harsh on you without even knowing you. It was really unfair and mean of me, and I'm really sorry."

"I already told you. Forgiven. You know my theory."

"I know, but it's still really nice of you. I've been holding on to so many grudges for so long, not forgiving even the people closest to me, and you don't know me from a hole in the wall, yet you're willing to give me a break. It's, like, I can't believe what a good person you are."

"Here's the thing, Neilly," he said softly. "I haven't always been such a good person. One of my biggest regrets is actually what a fuckup I used to be."

"Really? In what way?"

Griffin took a deep breath and dove in. "When my parents announced they were getting divorced, and then my mom took a nosedive, I was enough of a wreck—"

"I was just completely pissed off," I interrupted.

"And then when people found out why—"

"Were they just as brutal to you as they were to me?" I asked, wondering why I'd never realized what an ally I could've had in Griffin this whole time. I mean, we'd been through the same stuff. Things no one else could begin to understand.

"Yeah, it really sucked. I was trying to take care of things at home, getting in fights a lot at school, and lots of my so-called friends wouldn't even talk to me. So I started hanging around with kind of a rough crowd, got a Mohawk and dyed it blue, smoked pot all the time, drank in between classes . . . I don't know. I was just a mess."

"I dealt with it by shutting everyone out except my best friend, Lulu," I said. "I wouldn't hang out with anyone else. For a while, I wouldn't even go out on weekends because I just couldn't deal with what kids were saying. On the plus side, my grades got even better than they already were. . . ."

Griffin nodded. "So there I was. My mom was completely depressed, I'd stopped talking to my dad, and then my girlfriend Camilla broke up with me—she'd been kind of my rock up until then, but she couldn't deal with a guy who could barely communicate with her anymore because he was so wrecked all the time. I'd never felt so alone in my life, so I went ballistic, punching in a row of lockers until my hand was bloody and I'd broken two bones. At the time, I couldn't figure out why all these shitty things were happening to me. Now, of course, I can see how I was responsible for a lot of what went down. . . ."

"You can't beat yourself up over the past," I told him.

"I try not to anymore," he said. "Because the thing is, all those things I regret doing also led me to the things I am proud of doing now. My mom gave me a choice after the locker incident: go on a service trip or to a wilderness program for the summer. I picked the service trip and ended up working at a *comedor*—kind of like a soup kitchen—for little kids in Argentina. There were close to a hundred kids there every day, and my job was to play with them. That's it. Just play. These kids lived in houses made of scraps of stuff their parents had found lying around, and lots of them were abused, or from broken homes, or were, like, one of ten siblings. And all they wanted was some love and affection, so I gave as much as I could. It didn't take me long to realize that not only did I have so much more material stuff than these kids, but I also still had two parents who loved me more than anything in the world, regardless of whether they were divorced and my dad and your dad were together. And since then, I don't know . . . all the anger—it just kind of fell away. At the end of the summer, I came back here, fixed up my relationship with my dad, and started teaching ESL after school so I could keep going with the work I'd started in Argentina."

My mouth was pretty much hanging open by this point. Griffin was quite possibly the coolest guy I'd ever met. "So what happened to the blue Mohawk?"

He ran his hands through his awesome, choppy rock-star 'do. "It scared the kids, so I dyed it back to my natural color and grew it out."

"And what about Camilla? Did you guys ever get back together?"

"Nope. But we're kinda getting to be friends again, so that's a good thing."

"How'd you manage that one?" I asked, peeking across the room at Dec and Chantelle. They still looked entirely uncomfortable, like they were barely speaking.

"Time, mostly, to show her how much I'd changed," he said. "Well, that, plus I wrote her a kickass love song."

I imagined it must've sounded totally like a We the Kings tune. And that he'd sung it to her while staring deeply into her eyes. "Well, all I can say is, she's one lucky girl," I told him.

My life was getting more complicated than ever. But in a good way this time.

CHAPTER FIFTEEN

DECLAN

I FREAKING HATED SARAH. "OH, LET'S RECONNECT with our awkwardness and blahblahblah!" Chantelle would barely even look at me, much less speak to me.

"Look," I said, "I'm not like that."

Long pause. Interesting. The nonresponse appeared to be a way to say *bullshit* without actually saying it. I filed that away for possible future use. In the meantime, I fell back on my usual bad strategy: babbling.

"I mean. Look. I've been at community service, where I met this really cool vegan metal guy—wow, that sounded kind of gay, I mean, actually homosexual gay, not gay like stupid gay, not that I think gay is stupid, I mean, not with my family, not to mention my extended family. Right? I mean, so Neilly's dad is marrying a dude here—Roger is his name. Huge guy. Did that sound gay? Homosexual gay? Anyway, so, right, it's been a little bit of a stressful time in my life, you know, and that guy, Sam, well, we totally made up at community service, when I saved him from bullies by saying he was my boyfriend. Wow, that sounded gay again, didn't it? Okay. What I mean is this: I'm not a violent guy. It's not me, you know? I mean, yeah, it's something I did, but it's not who I am. I'm not proud of it. I'm actually pretty ashamed. I'm also totally ashamed that you were there when I had my first and only walk on the psycho side, because, yeah, you know, I wanted you to think I was dangerous in an alluring way, not in a cross-the-street-to-get-away-from-me way. You know?"

Chantelle still said nothing. I was pretty sure I saw her suppressing a smile the third time I thought I was sounding gay, though.

"Well, maybe you don't, because probably you have more common sense than I do, not to mention the fact that you probably don't have jocks riding you all the time—wow, that sounded unintentionally sexual. I meant riding in the sense of taunting, which—"

"Do you really think I don't have people taunting me?"

"Well, I mean, you're, like . . . you're not . . . why would they?"

"Oh my God, you're serious, and that's actually kind of sweet."

Sweet. I was so in. Babbling didn't work, so I was into listening now.

"What do you mean?"

"I mean, I'm, like, the only nonwhite face in the entire school. I mean, there are the normal, annoying, but ultimately harmless things, like the girls who can't stop asking me about my hair, the girls from the basketball team who keep asking me to try out, and a surprising number of girls who want to know if I've got an older brother—don't know what that's about—but anyway, there's all that stuff, the way everybody looks at me whenever anything black is mentioned in English class, like, *Hey, Chantelle, you want to read 'Still I Rise' for us? You're the black one, after all!* I freaking hate Maya Angelou!"

"Oh. I guess I never—"

"And the stupid guys who just happen to be singing 'Brown Sugar' every time I walk by? Do you think that doesn't make me want to kick someone until they die?"

"Well, I guess it probably would—"

"But I don't. That's the difference, Declan. My mom made it really clear to me from the time I could walk that the first time a guy raises his hand to you is the last."

"Well, technically, it was a foot, and I raised it to Sam, but—"

"I don't care, Declan. If you get violent when you're stressed out, how am I supposed to know what direction that violence is going to be aimed in next time?"

"Uh." It was a damn good argument. "I guess you can't."

And that was pretty much it until Neilly drove me home, blah-blahing the whole time about what an interesting guy Griffin was and obviously not thinking what I was thinking about—which was pulling the car over and making out just because we could.

The French, as Dad never tires of telling me, have a name for this: *l'esprit de l'escalier*—the spirit of the staircase. It's not a creepy transparent lady floating on stairs like they show on that ghost photographs show on TV, it's when you think of the perfect thing to say as you're walking down the steps after the argument.

Or, in my case, when your hot stepsister is driving you home. She was all happy about Griff, as she had started calling him, and I was pissed about that. The girl who understood and forgave me didn't even see me, and the girl who saw me didn't forgive or understand me. So I texted this to Chantelle: *If you wait for someone perfect you're gonna have a long wait.*

Mean, I guess, but with the memory of her out-arguing me ringing in my mind, and Neilly buzzing in my ear about another guy, I was feeling pissed. Which, I suppose, kind of illustrated Chantelle's point. And yet, I got this in return: *If I wait for someone better than you it wont be long.*

I laughed aloud, and Neilly looked hurt. "What? I mean, I'm sorry, but Sam and I have a history—"

"I'm sorry, it wasn't what you said. Chantelle just busted me. I think I'm in love. I sent her a nasty message because I was pissed about her basically saying I was an unredeemable psycho, and she just texted me back and totally busted me!"

Neilly looked at me. "And you're happy about this why?"

"Did you miss the part about how she texted me back?"

She smiled. "Gotcha. Abuse is better than neglect—is that the theory you're working on?"

"Hey, I've seen movies. I watch TV. I know hostile banter is just a cover for attraction."

"Uh, sometimes it's just hostility."

"Don't wreck my good mood, okay?"

"Okay. But so, what should I do? Should I listen to whatever Sam has to say? Or just keep blowing him off?"

"Forget him. You've got a hot guy right under your roof."

"Ew, no offense, but I don't think your dad is hot, and anyway, he's marrying my mom."

"Gross! I wasn't talking about my dad!"

"I know. Just busting on you."

Hey. Is that the kind of thing that masks attraction?

The exchange of text messages did not lead to a more general thaw with Chantelle. She still pretty much ignored me and just walked around looking hot. There was only this one single bright spot, and it was bright only as much as something that reveals the depth of my classmates' idiocy and cruelty can be.

So we were walking out of math class, and my ears were slightly more attuned to this since Monday, and I actually heard two morons going, "Deaw-de-ne-ne-neaaawww!" which was their attempt to sing the guitar part from the Rolling Stones' "Brown Sugar," which I had looked up the lyrics to, and, I mean, really, I can't believe Dad frets about death metal lyrics with that racist crap floating around.

I really had no desire to engage with the idiots, and I probably wouldn't have, except that I was kind of staring at Chantelle's butt at the time, because that's what I do when she is walking in front of me, and I noticed, up above her butt, that her shoulders tensed up. I thought about her wanting to kick somebody until they died, and how crappy it was to be picked on for just being who you are. And I did something stupid.

I got loud. First, I feigned a fit of hysterics until everyone in the hall was staring at me. I pointed at the two idiots, laughing really loudly and obnoxiously, and managed to choke out, "Oh . . . they're singing 'Brown Sugar'! Get it? 'Cause she's black! Ha! Oh, that's good stuff, guys. Funny . . ." Smiling, I wiped away imaginary tears, and the morons, as I'd hoped, turned their attention to me.

"Shut up, Columbine. What, are you tappin' that?"

"Nah, your mom keeps me pretty busy," I replied, and I know this is where the fist hits the face, and I really hoped Chantelle was watching me not square off to fight, just standing there like Gandhi offering nonviolent resistance. (Yes, I did study this stuff in social studies, and I know that it's supposed to involve brotherly love and not sarcasm and "yo mama" jokes, but, hey, one step at a time.)

I braced myself for the impact, and then something funny

happened. Nobody hit me. I opened my eyes and found myself staring at Sam's back.

"Cool it, guys," he said. "Chill out."

"But Columbine—"

"Gary. It's been a year. That joke was never funny, and it hasn't gotten any funnier. And neither has the 'Brown Sugar' thing. Come on, man, we've got a game on Saturday. Don't get suspended for this."

"Whatever," said Idiot No. 1, apparently named Gary, and he walked away. Idiot No. 2, apparently too much of a follower even to have a name, quickly followed. Sam turned around, smiled, said, "Now we're even, boyfriend," and walked away.

My phone vibrated, and I got this from Chantelle: *Thx*.

Well, it was something.

I sat down with Dad and Carmen and told them that I was really, officially going vegan, that after learning all this factory farm stuff, I really couldn't see myself eating animal products. (Also, I was hoping that even if Chantelle wasn't impressed by the rejection of violence that my vegan diet implies, there might be hot vegan girls around who see meat eating as a deal breaker, which would, of course, improve my odds tremendously.)

Dad sighed. "I— I'm not trying to be unsupportive here, but, what will you eat? Salad?"

"Actually, Ulf sent me all kinds of recipes, and there are cookbooks, and—"

Carmen jumped in. "Dec, I'll spring for the cookbooks if you help me do the cooking."

"Uh . . . okay." So the next day Carmen came home with a bunch of vegan cookbooks, and before I knew it, we were cooking all kinds of stuff, mostly Asian dishes, since those are pretty low in dairy to begin with, but also some stuff with silken tofu and nutritional yeast.

This stuff is, I guess, an acquired taste. But I like it because I don't have to hear screaming pigs in my brain while I'm eating it. Dad and Neilly wound up eating a lot of steaks and burgers that he "discreetly" grilled outside after they had picked over the dinner that Carmen and I made.

"I don't know if it's just being pregnant, but I swear to God, this stuff tastes awesome. I've been craving beets all day—can we make something with beets tomorrow?"

"Hell, yeah! How could I not like a vegetable that stains your poop blood-red?"

Neilly rolled her eyes. "Beets, Mom? Really? Why not just eat a shovelful of dirt?"

"If that's what your little sibling"—she patted her belly—"wants, that's what I'll eat. But right now, the order is for beets."

Neilly wanted help planning the big Halloween party, because, as she put it, "With this house, we need decorations somewhat weirder than the pumpkins and cats I'd come up with, but not as weird as the rotting corpses you'd probably like to have. I figure between the two of us, we'll come up with something workable."

Planning party decorations, even weird ones, is not high on my list of stuff to do. And the fact that these planning sessions always seemed to happen late at night, in Neilly's room, with her in pajamas (she favors fleecy bottoms and tank tops, but still) made it that much more torturous. Especially when we wound up in that too-tired-to-move, too-awake-to-go-to-sleep state and wound up talking about stuff beyond dry ice. (Oh hell, yeah, my Halloween party was gonna have dry ice. Are you kidding me?)

Like, for example, Neilly's seemingly eternal question: Should she listen to whatever Sam had to say to her, oh my God, he shut Gary up, that's so cool, he's really grown as a person, or would that be stupid for her to totally forgive him for macking on Lulu, that was so uncool, what kind of person would do that?

And I was like, "Well, I don't know, Neill"—I call her Neill 'cause we're close like that—"I mean, I guess it comes down to this: Does he have what you want in a guy?"

"I think so," she said. "I mean, I want somebody I can talk to." *Check. Got that—we're talking now.* "Somebody who makes me laugh." *Yup, several times a day.* "And somebody who's, you know, sensitive without being wussy." *I was pretty sure I had demonstrated that quality on several occasions.* "And, of course, someone who's smokin' hot."

Well, three out of four is 75 percent. Not great, but a solid passing grade. Something to build on.

CHAPTER SIXTEEN

Neilly

SOMETHING ABOUT GRIFFIN'S STORY, HIS TAKING A completely shitty, out-of-control situation and turning it into something great, made a big impression on me. Like, if he could change what he'd become—which was a pretty hurt and pissed-off person—then surely there was hope for me as well. Maybe I didn't have to be so defensive about everything anymore. Maybe I could just put down the armor, not worry so much about getting hurt all the time, and just be myself.

I decided to test out my theory the morning of the Halloween party.

I found *mi madre* in the nursery, stenciling cutesy little

yellow ducks in red raincoats onto the pale green walls. I stuck my head in the doorway. "Need help?"

This made her impossibly suspicious. "You need money for more haunted house decorations?" she countered.

"Can't I just do something nice for you without having an ulterior motive?"

She eyed me, looking for the catch. "You could, but that's not your normal MO these days. So what's up, honey? You okay?"

"I'm fine," I said. "Seriously, I only wanted to see if you wanted some help with Junior's digs. That's it."

"Why?" she finally asked, putting down her paints and brushes.

I shrugged. "I guess I feel bad about what a hard time I've been giving you lately."

This got her attention even more than my offer of help, no strings attached. "Thank you, Neilly," she said. "And let me apologize, too, while we're at it. No parent wants to think their choices have caused their children pain, but it happens. And I do blame myself for a lot of our problems lately."

Tears stung the corners of my eyes. "Mom, my being a bitch to you isn't your fault."

"No, but your being put through the ringer at school after your dad and I got separated . . . that certainly wasn't your fault. Your learning about Thomas and me in such an awkward way wasn't your fault, either. Not to mention finding out I was pregnant through Dec . . ."

So she really knew—and understood—how hard it had all been on me. This was a revelation in itself. Guess you can't hide as much as you think from dear old Mom. "It's okay, Mom. Really."

"I appreciate your saying that, Neilly."

"And I appreciate *you*," I told her. "Even though sometimes it might not seem like it, I do appreciate everything you do for me."

"Thanks," she said, giving me a kiss on the cheek. "I love you."

"I love you, too."

"And thanks for the offer, but I think this is a one-woman job," she said, shooing me out of the room. "I'll take you up on it next time."

When I got back to my room, I saw that Sam had given up on unanswered texts and had moved on to voice mail. *Took him long enough*, I thought. Lulu had jumped on that train almost immediately, and look where we were now: total BFFs again. Yet Sam and I still hadn't said a word since the big breakup.

I stared at the screen for a few seconds, debating whether I should listen to what he had to say at all, before I finally clicked onto the message:

"Hey, Neilly. I take it you're still mad at me, and I don't

blame you. But I want you to know how sorry I am for screwing things up between us, and how much I miss you. And if it's okay, I'd really like to talk to you at the party tonight. I mean, your party tonight. I mean, you know what I mean. Okay, see you later, babe. I love you."

It was sweet and infuriating and confusing all at the same time. Sweet because he was finally saying all the things he should've just said in the first place. Infuriating because it sounded like he assumed he was already back in my good graces, what with the "babe" and the "I love you" at the end of the message. And confusing because I wasn't sure what I wanted to do about that or how I felt about him at the moment.

With my mind still in a jumble of confusion, I decided to go see how Dec, the decorating committee, was doing. He'd had some completely rad ideas about how to make our Halloween party the most kickass bash of the year, with a blood-guts-'n'-gore fest that started in the attic and didn't stop until you got to hell (aka, the basement). It was the total pièce de résistance, a writhing sea of dismembered ghouls concocted out of dry ice, red goo made from borax, water, food coloring, and who knows what else.

I was so happy with the final product—and so hopped up on too many vanilla lattes—that I just couldn't contain my excitement. Dec was leaning against the back of the living room couch, admiring a particularly gruesome graveyard scene, when I went charging at him at full speed. "Thanks, bro! This is the coolest thing in the whole world!"

Though I had intended to send only Dec flying over the top of the couch, I misjudged my overly caffeinated strength and ended up going with him. We both landed with a plop on the other side, me on top of him, which must've hurt because he got all red in the face and his eyes practically bulged out of his head.

I found it all pretty hilarious. "Uh, sorry. I kind of only meant to knock you over—gently, of course—not knock the wind out of you," I said, cackling like one of our homemade attic-asylum inmates.

"No problem," Dec said, staring up at me with a dazed look in his eyes. "Hey, Neilly? Can I tell you something?"

He sounded so serious that he stopped my hysterics dead in their tracks. To make things even more uncomfortable, I'd just noticed there was something digging into my thigh. And even though I was 99.99 percent sure it was the hammer Dec had used to nail all the "lost souls" to our basement walls, I couldn't be positive. I was getting kind of worried that maybe he was thinking of nailing *me* with whatever it was.

So I extricated myself from the couch, stood up, and changed the subject as fast as I could. "Let me guess. You need to tell me I have something in between my teeth?"

A big, long, awkward silence. Then, finally, "Uh, yeah. Exactly."

Crisis averted. I ran my tongue along my front teeth and gave Dec an exaggerated smile. He gave me a thumbs-up, and suddenly everything was back to normal.

"You know, you wouldn't have this problem if you weren't sneaking dead cow meat with my dad all the time," he told me. "I mean, with the exception of broccoli, veggies are very friendly to dental hygiene."

"Thanks for the 411." I had no intention of changing my diet to include only the beets and roots and tofu blobs he and my mom ate now. Their cooking made the house smell like farts and dirt all the time—which was maybe okay for the blood-guts-'n'-gore Halloween party, but so not acceptable on a regular basis. "I better go floss and brush before people start getting here. 'Cause, you know, I might be getting some tonight."

"Serious?"

"Not a chance. How about you? You got any hot, vegan metal chicks coming to our little shindig?"

Dec grinned at me. "Hundreds of 'em, actually. I don't know how I'm going to juggle them all."

"I'm sure you'll manage," I said, wishing I could find him a real girlfriend to replace all the imaginary metal babes who seemed to inhabit his video games and imagination.

The rest of the night went by in a rush. Dec and I got into our costumes—I was a baby, complete with footie pajamas and a big pacifier; Dec was some kind of dead thing—and from there, the doorbell started ringing like crazy, and people just kept streaming in. Everyone loved how cool the decorations were, and I made sure they knew it was all Dec's doing.

I was in hell—otherwise known as the basement—listening to Ulf's band when they launched into an uncharacteristically mellow song. All of a sudden, no more screaming, an actual melody line, and lyrics you could really understand. I mean, the volume level had decreased so much that I could even make out conversation behind me.

"May I have this dance?"

I turned around to see Dec of the Dead holding his arms out to me.

"Sure thing," I said, and we started sort of shuffling around the room in circles. I made sure there was plenty of space between our bodies, just in case I'd been right about the hammer that maybe hadn't been a hammer at all.

"Having fun?" he asked.

I nodded. "Yup. You kick ass, bro."

"You think?"

"Absolutely. There's no way this party ever would've been as cool without you."

And then it was like his feet got stuck to the ground, and we stopped dancing. "I'm really glad to hear that, Neilly, because I feel the same way—"

Once again, whatever he had to say seemed serious. And once again, he didn't get a chance to spit it out because Griffin tapped him on the shoulder midsentence. "Mind if I cut in?"

"Oh . . . uh . . . sure," Dec said, his face clouding over into a scowl again. I felt bad that he hadn't gotten to tell me whatever was on his mind.

But the bad feeling quickly fell away as Griffin, who was wearing black skinny jeans, a WHERE THE WILD KINGS ARE hoodie, and yellow low-top Converse gathered me into what was essentially a movable hug.

"What are you supposed to be?" I asked, my heart beating even louder and faster than when I'd been in total caffeine overload that afternoon.

Griffin let his head rest on top of mine. "Travis, the lead singer from We the Kings. Everyone says I look like him, so I figured I'd take advantage of the resemblance. Plus, I'm kind of lazy about costumes."

"Tell me about it," I said, holding up the big-ass pacifier as proof.

And then we just kind of spun around and around. It was this great, suspended moment in time, which ended only because the band kicked into heavy death metal overdrive again. Moment over. Oh, well. At least Dec looked happy again, head banging away up at the front of the stage.

"Want to go grab some punch?" Griffin yelled over the noise.

"Sure," I yelled back.

So he grabbed my hand and led me out of the dance floor turned mosh pit.

We were still holding hands, even after we'd made our way upstairs to the living room, where all the food was set up. And I was thinking about never letting go, not even to fill up a punch cup, when we ran smack into Sam.

He stared at me, then at Griffin, then at our intertwined fingers, and did that puffing-his-chest-out/glaring thing that had always worked so well on the kids who were busting on me about my dad. Being on the receiving end of it, though, I just thought it made him look kind of ridiculous.

"Hey, Neilly," Sam said.

"Hey," I said, reluctantly letting my hand drop from Griffin's. "Uh, Sam, this is Griffin, my soon-to-be stepbrother."

Sam looked confused. "I thought the heavy metal guy was your stepbrother."

"Yeah, he is, too," I tried to explain. "Griffin is Roger's son. You know . . . my dad's . . . um . . . fiancé?"

"About that, Neilly," he said. "I'd be honored to take you to your dad's ceremony, just like you asked me to."

Griffin took my stunned silence as an excuse to extricate himself from the awkward situation. "Nice meeting you, man. I guess I'll see you at the wedding," he said to Sam. Then he touched my arm and said, "Neilly, I'm going back downstairs to check out the band's next set. Talk to you later, okay?"

I could only nod and watch him walk away. Damn, he had a cute butt.

"So what do you say, Neilly?" Sam asked, interrupting my lascivious thoughts about Griffin.

I turned my full attention to him and stuck my hands on my hips. "Why should I let you take me anywhere after what you did?"

"I know what I did was wrong, babe," he said. "I let all the shit my friends and my parents were throwing around get the best of me, and I'm not proud of caving like that. I guess I just thought I could get them off my back, show them what a man I was, by hooking up with someone else."

What flawed logic—like being an immoral person would make other people respect you more. "What kind of a man screws over someone he supposedly cares about?"

Sam shrugged. "I mean, a total asshole, I guess. But I was just so sick of them calling me a pussy-whipped fag. Neilly, I'm really sorry, and if it makes any difference, I totally realized none of that matters. What matters is that I love you, and I don't care what anyone else says about that, or us, or your dad. I just want to be with you."

Here's where I was supposed to melt, throw my arms

around his neck, and whisper, "I love you, too," so we could live happily ever after. So why was I just standing there, completely numb?

"Neilly, please," he said. If I didn't know him better, I'd think he was about to cry. "Just let me prove I'm for real by taking you to your dad's wedding. And we can see where it goes from there. No pressure, okay?"

I thought about Griffin's forgiveness theory and decided it was time to let another grudge go. "Okay," I heard myself saying.

I'd have to tell Dec later he was no longer obligated to be my mercy date. Now he'd be free to wear his corpse paint and listen to screamo with his friends all Saturday night instead of having to get in a penguin suit for me. He was sure to be relieved as hell.

And for the first time in recent history, I was at total peace with myself. I mean, at least I thought I was at total peace. Until Sam leaned over to kiss me, and all I could think was: *Wow, what would that have been like if it had been Griffin?*

When the last kid finally left, Ulf and the band had packed up and gone home, and nothing remained except some limp beet chips and dip, I made some tea and set out to relive the evening with my stepfrère. After much searching, I finally found Dec in his room, looking not at all like a guy who'd just thrown the best party in the history of our high school.

"What do you want?"

His words felt like an arctic blast, and I couldn't for the life of me figure out where his night had gone wrong. He'd been so happy head banging when I last saw him. "I . . . wanted to talk to you about how great the party was, but I guess now isn't the best time for that."

"Now is just as good as any time."

I figured he was bummed about girl stuff. Chantelle, probably. I thought maybe I could even help. "What's up your butt?" I asked, going for humor to lighten him up. "Your metal chicks turn into pumpkins before you got a blow job?"

He scowled. "Funny. Not."

"Seriously, Dec, what's the problem? Can I help?"

He wouldn't even look at me. "Don't think so. Especially since the problem *is* you."

"*I'm* the problem?" I asked, pointing to my chest, starting to get just as pissed at him as he seemed to be with me. "What's *your* fucking problem?"

"The problem is, you could have at least had the decency to let me know you no longer needed my services as your chaperone next weekend," he said, spitting the words out like nails. "I had to hear it from Sam."

I was thrown for a loop. Why did Dec care that I was letting him off the hook for our not-date? It didn't make sense. "I'm sorry, Dec. Sam practically begged me, and I figured you'd be psyched to be let off the hook—"

"I already rented a tux. You owe me seventy-five bucks. Cash only."

"Come on, Dec. I thought you'd be happy to have Saturday night to hang out with your friends—"

He gave me a stare that could turn hell into an icicle. "Well, you thought wrong."

CHAPTER SEVENTEEN

DECLAN

GIRLS.

This should have been the happiest night of my life. I hosted a party that was pretty well attended, despite the fact that all the invitations had said, "No Booze, No Drugs. Violators will be fed to the Thing Below." We didn't have to feed anybody to the Thing Below, nobody tried to sneak in booze, there were severed limbs everywhere, and I got tons of street cred from the school's scary/degenerate population because Slaughter of the Innocents had played *at my house.* Hell, even the hippies saw me in a new light when they found out the band was vegan.

So far, so good. But girls had to wreck it.

First, Neilly straddled me before the party. I mean, does she have no idea? No, I don't think she does, which is why I was about to tell her. Thank God I chickened out. Still, her tiny perfect body on top of mine is definitely an image going straight into the spank bank.

Then Chantelle didn't show up. This, despite her giving me a "maybe" response that I, perhaps too optimistically, interpreted as "I'll be there, and we'll totally make out."

I thought maybe I could break through Lulu's thinking of me as a sibling, but I kind of forgot about how girls love musicians. She spent the whole night about six inches from Slaughter of the Innocents, banging her head relentlessly and talking to Andy, the guitarist, every time the band took a break.

And then Sam approached me and told me it was a kickass party, and he was really sorry about misunderstanding everything, and he'd really learned a lot and was looking forward to going to the commitment ceremony with Neilly.

"Yeah, should be a good time," I said. "Well, enjoy the party— vegan non–pig in a blanket?" I said, offering him the appetizer tray.

"Uh, I'm gonna pass. I liked that punch with the brains in it, though."

"Cool!" I said, and disappeared into the chaos and banged my head some more.

Then Neilly came up to me after the party, and I was a dick to her.

I couldn't sleep, so I stayed up really late cleaning up. I slept in the next morning, and when I woke up, this note was pinned to my door: THX FOR CLEANING! YOU ROCK! —N

I crumpled it up and put it in my pocket and went downstairs for coffee. I had to make my own, since it was noon.

I was grinding beans when Neilly came in.

"Hey," she said.

"Hey," I answered. *"Feliz Día de los Muertos."*

"Um. What?"

"Day of the Dead. Big Mexican festival, you know? Skeletons?"

"I think I remember that from Spanish class. Anyway. Um. I'm sorry?" she said.

"Thanks."

"I mean, listen, Dec, I feel awful. I just thought—"

"See, I don't think you did. You didn't think . . . I mean, okay, I get it, I'm not—you can kiss me on the cheek and straddle me on the couch and stuff and not have the first idea of what that might be doing to me because you don't think of me as a real guy. I mean, okay, join the club, nobody else does, either, so why should you be different, and fine, right, I can live with that. I mean, it's like we're practically siblings, it would be weird, so it's probably just as well. I guess I just wish you had some small idea of the power you have as a beautiful girl, and that you'd be a little bit careful with that. But whatever, you've got low self-esteem, you put up with guys treating you like shit when you don't have to, you probably don't even get that. So fine, it's never gonna happen, it *was* never gonna happen, but I thought at least if you didn't think of me as a guy, you at least thought of me as a friend. Like, I thought we had some kind of bond here. . . . I mean, it's been nice to have an ally in the house and not just have it be me against the old people. But it turns out you don't even think of me as a friend. Right? Because you don't ditch friends that way. Right? Do you remember talking to me when you were so upset about that guy? And the first time he—not that he's such a terrible guy, but why would you give somebody a second chance to be a douche bag? You know? I mean, I'll give Chantelle that much—she told me straight out I wasn't getting another chance, and she stuck to it. At least she's got the balls to stand up for what she believes in. You . . . you just go running back to some guy who mistreats you. Do you really think he's learned his lesson? Here's the lesson he's learned: cheat on Neilly, get away with it. Do you honestly think he won't do it again? Or do you crave that kind of treatment? Do you, like, hope he's going to cheat on you because you think you deserve it? Or are you just completely spineless?"

Fortunately the teapot was whistling by this point, so I put the beans into the French press, turned off the stove, and poured the hot water over the beans. I looked up and saw Neilly was crying.

"That's a really horrible thing to say," she said quietly.

"Yeah, well, the truth hurts, I guess."

She ran from the room, and I sat there and felt horrible. It didn't make me feel better to have her be sad. Weird. I thought if

I really let her have it, I would kind of transfer all my bad feelings to her. Instead, I kept mine and gave her some, too. Well, too bad. She deserved it.

I pressed the coffee down and poured the bitter black elixir into the mug Carmen had given me as a housewarming gift. On one side it read, I LIKE MY COFFEE BLACK . . . and on the other side was a grinning Satan holding a cup of coffee, with the words LIKE MY METAL!

I took my coffee and went to the computer to send Ulf a little thank-you e-mail, since they'd played for free, which they totally didn't have to do. Ulf had beaten me to it, though.

"Declan—I just wanted to thank you for the opportunity to play last night. We sold twenty CDs, which is twice as many as we've ever sold at a gig. And fifteen T-shirts, which is just like free money at this point. Some kid at your party said his dad books the VFW and could get us booked for an all-ages Sunday show. It's pretty discouraging trying to make music sometimes, and we really feel like we're on our way for the first time. So thanks. PS—check our Facebook."

Wow. I thought I was scamming free live music. I didn't know I was doing a public service. I checked the Slaughter of the Innocents Facebook page, and found my picture prominently displayed. "This is the coolest person in Oak Heights. Except us, of course," it said in the news section, which went on to talk about what a killer party I threw and that I had balls to stand up against unthinking alcohol and drug use and how I made kickass vegan appetizers as well. (Carmen actually made most of the vegan appetizers, but I wasn't going to quibble.)

I had twenty friend requests. I accepted them all, thus making real people outnumber bands on my friend list for the first time ever. Twelve of the twenty were female. Four of the twelve girls were smokin' hot. Five others I would classify as pretty. The other three were female.

Maybe things were looking up.

Dad came in and peeked at the computer screen as I was perusing the photo albums of one "veganchick17."

"Is that SuicideGirls?" he asked.

"Dad, I'm gonna ignore the fact that you not only know the name of a porn site but know that it features tattooed hotties like veganchick17 here, and tell you proudly that this is an unpaid encounter, that this girl wanted to friend me because Slaughter of the Innocents said I was cool. Also, I don't know if you get this from the handle, but she's seventeen."

"Hey, that's great. Listen, Dec, I just wanted to thank you for the job you did cleaning up. I really thought we'd be spending the whole day today digging out from your party, but the place looks—well, not great, but not really any worse than it did before the party."

"We aim to please."

"Anyway, Dec, listen, Sarah's running a special Day of the Dead thing this afternoon. You wanna go? There'll be skeletons . . ."

"And . . . ?"

"And I'm gonna say a little something about your mom. What do you say?"

"I say that sounds like it would make me really sad. Pass."

Dad looked pained, like he was about to say something, but he held it back, whatever it was. "All right, Dec. I'm not gonna force it."

"Sweet. Have fun."

"Yeah, I don't really think it's the kind of thing you classify as fun, but I appreciate the sentiment."

"Cool."

I retired to my room to play Xbox and feel sorry for myself. Which worked fine for a while, but I eventually got stuck at one point on level twelve for like half an hour, and I knew I just needed to turn off the Xbox and try again later. Also, I knew I had been mean to Neilly just to hurt her, and I felt kind of bad about it. That's not true. I felt horrible about it. I pretty much felt horrible about everything.

I hadn't really eaten anything, which couldn't have helped my mood, so I wandered downstairs for a snack.

Carmen was sitting at the table with probably two pints of Ben and Jerry's in a mixing bowl in front of her. She looked up kind of guiltily at me, but I couldn't very well give her any shit about her dairy consumption when she was the person who'd been most supportive of my vegan ways.

"Hey, Carmen. How's Junior?" I asked.

She laughed. "Junior is demanding a whole lot of Chunky Monkey today."

"Sweet."

"Yeah, the soy stuff just wouldn't do."

"Carmen, I don't expect you to go vegan, you know."

"I know. I just . . . I don't want you to think I'm not being supportive."

"Are you kidding me? You're the only other person who eats the stuff I make!"

"Yeah. Well, it tastes really good. So how are you doing?"

"Honestly? I feel like a piece of crap."

"Lot of that going around today. Neilly said more or less the same thing before she left."

"She said I was a piece of crap? I'm not really surprised. I pretty much deserve that."

"No, I mean, she said she felt horrible."

"Yeah. I guess that's my fault. Where'd she go?"

"She went to the Day of the Dead thing with your dad." *Well, that was weird.* "I guess—so you guys had some kind of fight or something?"

"Or something. It's actually pretty embarrassing. I don't feel like talking about it. I don't . . . I mean . . . I don't know what the . . . I just feel totally lost right now. You know? I just want to be happy, and I guess I don't know how. I kind of thought that having a girlfriend or whatever . . . I don't know, like the girl I thought I liked didn't show up last night, and Neilly had told me to give up on her ages ago, which I guess I should have done, but anyway. It's like, I scared Chantelle away by being angry, and Neilly's been, like, my best friend, like the person my age who's really stood by me, and now I was a dick and drove her away by being angry. And I'm always barking at Dad. I'm too . . . I'm mad all the time, and I kind of like it, you know, but it gets . . . I guess I'm just tired. Does that make sense?"

"Yeah. I think so." She ate a bite of Chunky Monkey. "I know this is kind of a dumb question, but is it just your mom that you're mad about? I mean, this"—she gestured around the room with her spoon—"this was a big change that we sprang on you, and I know it's got to be—"

"No. Dad was right about that. It's better. It's more fun." I paused for a minute. "I guess I should maybe tell him that."

"He'd appreciate it."

"Yeah. Well. Anyway, I guess, yeah, I'm mad about mom. I just . . . It's not fair that so many people who suck are still alive and my mom is dead. It's not fair that other people take their moms for granted and I'll never get to know mine at all, not really, I mean, not like who she was besides being a little kid's mom." And now I started to cry. "I mean, you know? It's not fair. None of it's fair. I miss her. You know? I mean, I'm happy for you guys, I actually am, and you can tell Dad I said that because I'm probably too chickenshit to say it myself, and I'm glad for Junior that he's going to have two parents. I just miss my mom. I want my mom back, and she's never ever coming back."

My head was down on the table now, and Carmen put a hand, freezing from holding the bowl of ice cream, on the back of my head. It felt good. "I'm so sorry, sweetie," she said.

"And"—my head was still on the table, and I was talking tearfully at the wall—"I don't want to be mad all the time, you know, but I just don't want to . . . It's like being mad about Mom being dead is the only thing left that connects me to her. It feels like I'd be betraying her if I stop."

Carmen rubbed my head some more with her freezing-cold hand. I guess that's, like, a thing moms do. It was really nice. But it made me cry more. "Sweetie," she said, and I didn't mind her calling me that, "do you think your mom would want you to be mad forever?"

"I don't know if I can help it," I said.

"Well," she said, "I have an idea."

She told me her idea. It was so incredibly awesome, I couldn't believe I'd never thought of it myself.

"Dad will kill us both. I can't be responsible for you guys breaking up before Junior's even born," I said.

"Don't be a pussy," she said, and I was suddenly just thrilled to have this woman in my life. It started out pretty shitty, but this might just be the best Day of the Dead ever.

CHAPTER EIGHTEEN

Neilly

DEC DIDN'T STOP BEING A DICK TO ME AFTER THE night of our party. Instead, he continued being a dick right on into the next day, to the point where he made me cry. In fact, it seemed like that was his main intention.

Stupid, huh?

But I guess he thought I was the one who was stupid. For letting him off the hook for my dad's commitment ceremony. Like I should've known it would matter to him. Dec got all high and mighty, told me I was a crappy friend, that I didn't even see him as male or human—or something, I don't even know—and that I let myself be treated like shit by everyone because I have low self-esteem.

If there was anyone with low self-esteem in the room, I didn't think it was me. Not that I bothered to say that. Because I was so floored.

Before the verbal spew he puked all over me, I had been under the impression that Dec and I had gotten to be friends. Maybe even really good friends.

Turns out he's just another dick in disguise.

We'd been having, like, pajama parties in my room every night, talking about anything and everything, and instead of actually listening to me, all he was thinking about was sex, my boobs, and whatever other kind of perverted crap goes on in guys' minds. All because I kissed him on the cheek once, and accidentally fell on top of him after we made the house all Halloween-y. Or at least I think that's what he was trying to tell me, among other mean stuff, during that whole diatribe.

And so I guess it really wasn't a hammer in his pocket after all.

Ick.

When I told Sam about it, his response was, "See? That's why guys and girls can't be friends."

"What? Why not?"

"Because the girl thinks everything is all platonic. And the whole time, the guy is thinking, *I wonder if I can get into her pants yet.* And that's why mixed-gender friendships never work."

His pronouncement made me sadder than ever. Now not only couldn't I be friends with Dec, but I couldn't be friends with half of the Earth's population. And how depressing is that?

So I'd spent the week avoiding my future stepbrother, ex-friend. Every time he saw me, he'd give me these puppy dog eyes like I should apologize or something. But I really didn't think I needed to apologize for anything, especially seeing as the last time I did, look what it got me. Ripped a new a-hole.

In addition to his pathetic looks, Dec also seemed to be spending a lot of time being a big baby about some little scrape or something he had on his arm. It was covered up in gauze, and he kept touching it and wincing like he had gangrene and they'd be amputating soon. I guess I was supposed to ask if he was okay, but I wasn't about to give him the satisfaction.

The big bully was nothing but a wussy.

Make that a big, perverted wussy.

Thank God he wasn't going to be my escort to the wedding. Now I wouldn't have to worry about accidentally giving him a boner or his looking down the front of my dress if I happened to lean over for something.

No surprise, we still weren't speaking by the time Saturday rolled around. The day of my dad's wedding had finally come, and I was just finishing up my hair—wash, condition, air-dry until just damp, blow-dry, add thermal product, spank it with a flat iron until it's pin straight—when the doorbell rang. I checked myself in the mirror and deemed what I saw as good. Very, very good. My fuchsia Betsey Johnson dress was a great mix of funky and flirty, my makeup was dramatically different than my daytime look, which consisted of nothing but ChapStick, cover-up, and eyeliner, but subtle enough that I didn't look like some weird, painted china doll, and my heels were sexy yet still walkable. All in all, I was pleased as hell.

So imagine my shock when I opened the door and saw Sam, not in a tux and holding a corsage but in a T-shirt, shorts, and high gym socks and holding a beer can, looking very much like Paulie Bleeker from *Juno*.

I just stood there, mouth hanging open, staring at fake Paulie Bleeker clutching an all-to-real Bud, and for one of the first times in my life, I was left completely speechless. I truly had no words for the travesty in front of my face.

Sam semi-leaned, semi-fell against the door frame. "Wow, Neilly. I've never scheen you look scho beautiful."

My formerly paralyzed tongue suddenly went into action. Probably loosened up by all the alcohol Sam was breathing my way. "Wow, Scham. I've never scheen you scho drunk. Or dishgushting."

He leaned into kiss (kissch?) me, but I backed away.

"Awww, come on now, Neilly. Don't be mad at me."

I could not believe the guy's gall. Was I supposed to be happy he'd come to pick me up for our date to my dad's wedding piss-drunk in a *Juno* costume?

"Sam, why don't I drive you home so you can take a quick shower? I'll pick you up a double shot at Starbucks while you're getting ready, and we can forget this whole scene ever happened."

Sam shook his head as if to clear it. It seemed to work, at least a little bit, because when he opened his mouth again, the slurring was under control.

"Yeah, see, here's the thing, Neilly," he said, lifting his index finger to the sky, like God himself was about to make the pronouncement. "My dad is really not cool with me going tonight. In fact, he forbids it. I tried to talk some sense into him, but he said it's a crime against nature, and that I can kiss the season good-bye if I do."

"It's a crime against nature to escort me to my dad's wedding?" I demanded. "And he won't let you play any more football this year if you do? That's the stupidest thing I ever heard!"

Sam put his hands on my shoulders. The fact that he leaned too much of his weight on me reminded me once again of his ultra-inebriated state. "Neils, I can't *not* play."

I was losing my patience. "I really don't think your dad would go through with it, Sam. Be realistic."

Sam shrugged. "You know I'd do just about anything for you, Neilly. . . ."

"Clearly not," I said quietly. "I mean, you won't even stand up to your dad for me."

Sam stared down at his shoes, then back up at me. His eyes were all watery, but I couldn't tell if he actually felt bad about doing such a horrible thing or if he was just glassy-eyed from all that drinking. "Neilly, please. I already stood up to him, and he wouldn't budge. I love you. But I just can't go."

"You don't love me," I growled. "You never did. Love isn't a part-time thing, where you get to be around for the easy stuff, the fun stuff, and then completely bail on the hard stuff. Love isn't cheating and hoping you won't get caught. Love isn't showing up in some stupid freaking seventies sweat socks when you're supposed to be in a tux. And love isn't having to get shitfaced so you can tell me you don't have the balls to take me to a same-sex wedding, because you and your dad are freaked out that you'll somehow become gay by association. You don't deserve to even talk to me, much less tell me you love me."

That's when I slammed the door in his face. Sam knocked on the window a few times to try to get my attention, but I pulled the curtains shut. Eventually, he shrugged and walked away, taking swigs off his Bud every few steps.

I knew I was really going to have to suck it up and put on a happy face, despite the fact that all I wanted to do was scream and cry and freak out. My dad and Roger were counting on me, and I was due at the church in fifteen minutes.

210

I texted my mom from where I stood. The prospect of walking up all those stairs to her and Thomas's room was just too overwhelming at that moment. *Can I grab a ride with you guys?*

Sure. Won't even ask why, she shot right back.

I plunked down on the couch, my chin in my hands, and tried just to breathe. In, out, in, out. It was a humongous effort, but eventually my anger started to fade a little bit.

And who knows how long later, I felt a plop on the couch next to me. I glanced over, expecting to see my mom, but it was Dec. In a tux. "I'm not afraid of your dad's gayness rubbing off on me, so if you still need an escort, I'm all yours."

I gave Dec a pathetic little smile that probably looked more like a wince. "You heard, huh?"

He nodded. "Every last word."

"That's just icing on the humiliation cake," I said, closing my eyes like maybe that might make me invisible and, therefore, not publicly mortified.

"The only person who should feel humiliated is Sam," he told me. "Well, and his dad, too. But you? You should be proud of yourself."

"Huh?"

"I mean, I am. Proud of you, that is," he said. "And I take back everything I said last week. You really stood up for yourself with Sam. And I loved your whole 'love isn't' spiel. It was, like, straight out of a romantic comedy."

"Except those usually have happy endings," I pointed out.

"So maybe this will, too."

"Hey, Dec? I'm really sorry."

"Me, too. About everything. I was a complete asshole."

"Me, too," I said, grinning. "Friends?"

"Friends," he said, grinning right back at me.

CHAPTER NINETEEN

DECLAN

SO LIFE IS PRETTY WEIRD.

I yelled at Neilly for being spineless, and then I was the one too chickenshit to apologize first.

"Listen," I said, "I just . . . If I . . . I don't want you to worry all the time about my perviness or anything."

She laughed. "I'm not worried about it. I'm just aware of it. I think it's probably better that way, don't you?"

"Yeah, I guess so. So, um, I've got a lot to catch you up on. I just . . . I've . . . I don't want this to sound creepy or anything. But I've just missed you. I know I went off on you, but you are a good friend. Actually, you're probably the best friend I've ever had. And I want you to still be my fri— no, I want you to be my sister."

She smiled. "Yeah. We can do that. But if we're going to be real siblings, we have to be able to hug once in a while without you getting all . . ."

"Erect?"

"Yeah. Exactly."

"I think I can handle that. I've got a couple of . . . Well, I have to start at the beginning."

Just then the car pulled up, and Dad honked the horn. "Okay, well, we have to go," Neilly said. "Come on. You can tell me in the car."

Into the backseat we went, and Dad was all fretful. "Everything okay? I mean, are you guys all right? I thought—Dec, you were supposed to . . . And Neilly, what about—"

Carmen put a hand on his arm. "They're here. They're fine. We're fine. Now let's go watch my ex-husband marry a dude."

God, Carmen is so cool.

"So," Neilly said. "You were going to tell me the whole story."

I looked nervously at the front seat. "Uh. Well. Maybe you should, um, ah, maybe when we get there"—I kind of nodded my head at Dad—"I can talk more freely, and—"

"Dec, just spill it," Carmen said. "He's got to find out some time."

"Find out what? What are you guys talking about? Is this . . . Oh God, what is it. Dec, did you get arrested again and not tell me?"

I laughed. "Keep that image in your mind, Dad, so when you

hear the real story, it won't freak you out so much."

"Freak me out? What? What's going to freak me out?"

"Dec, you're making it worse. Tell the story," Carmen said, smiling.

"Okay. So last Sunday, after having been a total dick, I was crying in the kitchen, and Carmen here talked to me, and Dad, you got a bargain here, 'cause I got better therapy from her than I have gotten from Dr. Gordon, but anyway . . . I told her how I was tired of being mad all the time."

"Yeah, we're all tired of your being mad all the time," Dad said, smiling. Score one for the old man.

"Anyway, Carmen had this great idea, so she used her graphic design mojo to help me make this mock-up of what I wanted, and then she signed the form as my parent, even though, you know, legally—"

"*What* form?" Dad asked.

"Honey, watch the road. Let Dec tell the story," Carmen said. She was enjoying this almost as much as I was.

"I really wanted to sign my name as *Stig Costello*, which I've decided to adopt as an alias should the need ever arise, but Carmen said I should just do it in a completely aboveboard way."

"Do *what*?" Dad and Neilly both screamed.

"Jinx," I said. "Dad, Neilly, you owe me a vegan smoothie. I prefer mango. Anyway . . . Dad, watch the road, for God's sake, will you? I lost one parent in a car wreck, let's not make it two or three."

"Sweetie," Carmen said, patting Dad's arm, "just pull over for the end of the story."

"Did you just make a joke about your mom's death?" Dad asked.

"Yeah, I guess so," I said.

"Wow. So now you're admitting it happened, if only in a sort of twisted way. Good deal." Damn it. Score another one for the old man.

"So, Stig," Neilly said. "What form did you sign?"

"So glad you asked, my sister. The form that one signs when one goes to get a tattoo."

"A *what*?" Dad and Neilly both screamed again.

"My new friend Anastasi—aka veganchick17, who, by the way, I'm meeting for coffee before the SOI show at the VFW next week—is, as you recall from the SuicideGirls comparison you made, Dad, rather heavily inked, in addition to bespectacled and delicious, so I inquired of her where one might go for such a thing. She sent me to a very nice place—all vegan, by the way. Did you know some tattoo inks have animal products in them? How gross is that?"

"Let's see it," Neilly said. "That's why you've been babying your arm all week, right? Let's see it!"

I looked forward at Dad. He kept looking back at me and sideways at Carmen. "You knew about this?" he asked Carmen. "He's sixteen! Dec, when you get to be my age—"

"I'm still gonna be stoked as hell to have this on my arm," I said, removing the tuxedo jacket and rolling up my sleeve.

"Oh my God," Dad and Neilly both said, but I'm not sure if that one counted as a jinx, since Neilly's was, like, "Oh my God, how cool is that," and Dad's was more in the "Oh my God, my kid has a big ass tattoo on his arm vein."

I looked down at my tattoo. No skulls, no demons, nothing anybody would remotely expect from me. Instead, a single lily, and above it, PATIENCE. Now I'll always be connected to Mom because her name is on my arm. And yeah, if it reminds me to take a deep breath before I get mad, well, I guess that's okay, too.

"You are the coolest person I know," Neilly said.

"You act like you don't know your own mom," I said.

"Apparently, I don't!" Neilly said, laughing. "Knocked up, hanging out at tattoo parlors . . . Mom, do you want me to drop you guys at the mall so you can hang out by the fountain and go shopping at Hot Topic?"

"Not tonight, sweetie. I have to watch your father marry a dude, remember?"

"Right."

"Dad?" I said. Dad still had this stunned look on his face. At least, I think it was stunned. I realized it might be something else when I saw the tears start leaking out of his eyes.

"It's really beautiful," he choked out in this semi-crying voice.

"Aw, sweetie, I'm sorry," Carmen said, stroking Dad's arm.

He takes a minute to collect himself. "Don't be," he says. "I just . . . I just got overwhelmed with how lucky I feel. That's all."

There was a moment of uncomfortable silence, which I was trying to think about how to break when Dad—Dad! What's the world coming to?—suddenly collected himself and said in a chipper voice, "Now, are you ready to go watch your ex marry a dude?"

"Totally," Carmen said, and the two of them gazed at each other so lovey-dovey that I thought I might puke.

"Hey, Dad, try to keep it in your pants till we get home, willya?"

Neilly hit me really hard on the tattoo—which was still kind of tender—when I said this, and I was yowling in pain, and Dad said, "Thank you, Neilly. All right, family. Let's go to a wedding."

CHAPTER TWENTY

Neilly

MY DAD WAS PACING NERVOUSLY IN THE BACK OF AUNT Sarah's crazy little church—pretty much where this whole story started—by the time we got there.

"Neilly!" he exclaimed, running his fingers through what was left of his thinning hair. "Where've you been? I was so worried—"

"I'm here now, Dad. You know I wouldn't miss this for the world."

While my mom, Thomas, Dec, and the rest of the stragglers found seats in the crowded pews, I stayed behind in the vestibule with my father. He'd asked me to be his person of honor, and, quite frankly, I was extremely honored by his asking me to do so.

I could feel a lump rising up in my throat as the opening bars of Pachelbel's Canon rang out, but I tried to joke my way out of totally losing it. "So how'd you get to be the bride in this equation?" I whispered to my dad as we step-together-step-togethered down the aisle.

"Have you seen my husband-to-be?" he whispered back, and we both had to stifle really inappropriate giggles.

Roger stood waiting for my dad at the front of the church, looking like he was about to faint. And so *his* person of honor—Griffin—put an arm around his dad to steady him, and I thought it was the sweetest gesture an unconventional wedding had ever seen. Especially knowing how long it had taken both of us to get where we were, emotionally speaking, about the whole thing.

When we finally made it to where they stood, my dad and Roger fell into this huge embrace. And when the hug ended, Roger held both my dad's cheeks and gave him a kiss. That's when everyone in the church kind of exploded in applause, hooting and hollering and woo-hoo-ing.

"Love makes a family!" I heard someone yell.

"Go Dad and Roger!" Lulu piped in. She'd known my dad since we were little, so she was entitled to call him that.

"Down with labels, up with love!" her date, Andy, the SOI guitarist, added.

Dec put two fingers in either side of his mouth and whistled.

"And I didn't even say, 'You may kiss your spouse' yet," Aunt Sarah quipped.

Things calmed down considerably after that. Aunt Sarah said all the usual great stuff, like how God loves everyone regardless of race, creed, nationality, or sexual orientation—she was preaching to the choir here, as probably three-quarters of the church was packed with same-sex couples—and how special my dad and Roger's love was. And then she really *did* say "You may kiss your spouse," and then they smooched, and everyone went crazy again, and it was just the coolest thing ever.

At the reception, Dec and I were dancing to some totally corny eighties song when I just had to get back to the subject of his ink. I felt like his moment of glory had been cut short in the car, and he deserved some serious props. Well, he and my mom, that is.

"Dude, have I told you lately how awesome that tattoo is?" I asked, patting his arm more gently this time.

Dec just grinned. "Uh, I don't know if you know this, but my mom's name was Patience. So it kind of means a lot to me. Like, I know I won't ever forget her, 'cause she'll always be here with me."

I nodded, the tat even cooler now that I knew how much meaning was behind it. "You know, I've been thinking. Would you mind it very much if I copied you?"

"I wouldn't mind, but I also don't think you'd look very

good with a flowered tattoo that says 'Patience' on your bicep," he said.

"Don't worry, I've got my own message and spot in mind," I told him. "You're just the inspiration."

"So you're saying I inspire you?"

I nodded. "I guess I am."

"If you had asked me at the beginning of this year what one thing I never thought I'd hear you say, that would've been it," he said. "Come to think of it, I guess I never thought I'd hear you say anything. To me, that is."

"Well, I'm glad I did."

"Me, too."

Bret Michaels was just about taking it home, singing about some chick who had a thorn in her rose, when Griffin tapped Dec on the shoulder. "May I?"

It was déjà vu all over again. Except this time Dec surprised me by agreeing to bow out with a smile.

But I shook my head. "We'll finish out this dance, and then I'll come find you, okay?"

Griffin nodded. "I'll be out on the balcony."

"You didn't have to do that, Neilly," Dec said once Griffin had walked away.

"Yes, I did," I told him. "You ripped me a new one about not being a good friend last week, and I don't want to make the same mistake twice."

Dec opened his mouth and closed it a few times, but nothing came out.

"What?" I asked him.

"Uh, except when it comes to Sam, I guess," he finally spit out, totally cracking himself up.

"Huh?"

"He was the same mistake twice, wasn't he?"

"Touché, brother. Touché. I won't do it again."

"Don't," Dec said. "He doesn't deserve a great girl like you."

I smiled up at my new stepbro. "Thanks. For everything."

"Right back at ya, sista."

When I finally found my way back to Griffin much later on, things were just about wrapping up at the reception. "Sorry we didn't get to talk much tonight," I told him. "It was so crazy in there with my dad wanting to introduce me to all his friends, you know. . . ."

"Totally. So maybe we can hang out tomorrow afternoon instead? Grab a coffee or something?"

"Sure," I said. But then remembered I already had afternoon plans. "Actually, can we make it tomorrow night?"

By the time I met my very hot, not-really-stepbrother-since-gay-unions-are-still-not-legally-recognized-in-the-backward-state-I-live-in the next night for coffee, I was a changed woman. And I couldn't wait to show Griffin the new me. So right after giving him a big hug hello, I peeled back the gauze protecting the new tat I'd just gotten inked on the inside of my wrist.

Griffin broke out into a huge smile when he saw what it was: a delicate little pink heart surrounded by the words *Love will find a way* in fancy script.

"I couldn't agree more," he said, and proceeded to plant the most warm and soft, sweet and lingering kiss in the world on me.

And let me tell you, it was totally smokin'.

EPILOGUE

DECLAN

THINGS DIDN'T EXACTLY WORK OUT WITH ANASTASIA. Somebody got a little too clingy after things got physical. And yeah, that somebody was me. I may have professed my undying love. The details are a bit hazy. Or, anyway, I'm trying to make them get hazy, because otherwise I can still feel the humiliation.

But it wasn't all bad. For one thing, please note that I said *after* things got physical. Five times. The fourth and fifth of which actually lasted longer than thirty seconds. For another, we had a great time together for the couple of months we were together, and being seen in public with a girl, especially one as completely smokin' hot as Anastasia, announced to the world that I was boyfriend material. Neilly tried to explain this to me, but I didn't understand it at all because it has to do with the way the female brain works. But in a nutshell, if a guy sees a girl with another guy, he gets annoyed because she's off-limits. If a girl sees a guy with another girl, he automatically goes into the potential boyfriend file.

I know. I don't get it, either.

But it doesn't matter because once Anastasia and I broke up (Okay, after she dumped me. There may have been tears. There may have been some rather embarrassing and unmanly pleading. . . .), I had like three girls suddenly sending me messages on the old social networks. Even Chantelle started talking to me again. Too bad for her—she had her chance.

So I've got three prospects right now, or four, I guess, if you count Chantelle, which I don't, probably, and I don't feel particularly desperate to have a girlfriend right now, which probably will attract even more girls.

I will now stop talking about girls because it's about to lead to me bragging about some of the various activities Anastasia and I engaged in, particularly on occasion four, and apparently people get really annoyed and/or disgusted when you brag about such things.

And, anyway, there was another big event that took place after Neilly's dad's wedding.

I got this text from Dad during fifth period: *Carmen's in labor. Come to the hospital after school.*

This was followed almost immediately by one from Neilly: *No f-n way are we waiting till after school. Meet me in the hall.*

So we excused ourselves from class and went straight to the hospital. I figured we could probably talk our way out of it, and if not, detention was better than sitting in biology class trying to memorize the stupid photosynthesis formula while my little sibling was entering the world.

But of course we got to the hospital and nothing much was happening. Dad popped out of the delivery room and announced that Carmen was fully dilated. "Like, her pupils or something?" I asked.

"Her cervix, idiot," Neilly said, and, I mean, I like Carmen a lot—I may even love her in a totally parental kind of way—but I really wasn't interested in any more updates on her lady parts.

Which was good, because Dad then disappeared for an hour and a half. Neilly and I sat there doing nothing, bored out of our minds from waiting and yet too excited to focus on anything. Here's how bad it was: I couldn't even read the sex columns in the women's magazines.

I worried and fretted until Neilly got sick of it and barked, "Will you stop pacing, sit down, and shut the hell up? Everything is fine!"

And it was. Dad came out looking as haggard as I can remember seeing him, tears running down his face, and said, his voice breaking with emotion, "So do you guys want to meet your little sister, or what?"

"Ha!" Neilly said. "Sister! In your face!"

We went into the room and Carmen, all flushed and sweaty, was holding our baby sister. Who was, of course, perfect and beautiful. "Dec, Neilly, this is Ramona."

"Oh my God, Mom! That is so sweet!" Neilly said, then turned to me and said, "We read every single Ramona book together when I was little. Mom used to read them to me at bedtime."

Well. She could think what she wanted, but I knew my little sister was named after a Ramones song. The only thing cooler would have been if they had named her Lemmy, but you really can't do that to a girl.

Neilly held her for a while, then passed her over to me. "Support her head, Dec," Dad coached. I figured he'd just been through a lot, so I did not remind him that he'd instructed me on the proper way to hold a baby, like, eight million times in the last two weeks.

I held my baby sister in my arms, and she was so light and warm and sweet and perfect, and at that moment I really just wanted to protect her from everything in the whole world—from hurt and fear and pain and grief and everything bad.

But, of course, you can't protect anybody from everything bad. Not even my little sister Ramona. All you can do is hope she's tough enough to get through the bad stuff. I figured Ramona might need the toughness more than I did at that point, so I pulled the pin off my shirt and stuck it on Ramona's onesie, while

Dad squealed about a sharp object being so near to her.

I handed Ramona back to Carmen, and there she was, my little sister, badass-in-training, named after a Ramones song and sporting a Minor Threat pin before she was even an hour old.

We hung out for a while, but then Dad and Carmen and sweet, sweet little Ramona needed some sleep, so they booted Neilly and me out.

We argued in a good-natured way about whether Ramona was named after some girl in books or a Ramones song, and about whether she was going to be a badass or a girly-girl, but since I knew I was right on both counts, I let it drop.

We stopped at the store, got some mango smoothie ingredients, and went back to the Mansion of Metal. Or, as our family likes to call it, home.

ACKNOWLEDGMENTS

Trish thanks:

Steve-o, for being my lifelong partner in crime; Courtney, for being such an inspiration; Kelsey, for always making me laugh; my mama, for always being on my side; Charlotte, for being my twin from another mother; Holly, for being cool like that; Greg, for his enthusiastic support; and Suzanne, for being my BFF all these years and encouraging me to write with her awesome and awesomely talented husband Brendan (and a special shout-out to both of them for letting me play guitar at their wedding).

BRENDAN THANKS:

Suzanne Demarco, for support, inspiration, and for introducing me to my coauthor; Greg Ferguson, for editorial awesomeness; Doug Stewart, for continuing friendship, support, and agential awesomeness; Casey Nelson, Rowen Halpin, and Kylie Nelson, for inspiration and support; and Trish Cook, for being so much fun to work with.

Trish Cook is the author of *So Lyrical* and *Overnight Sensation*. In her real life she's a communications consultant, but for fun she writes songs, runs marathons, tries out for random reality shows, and plays guitar and sings for The Holly Llamas, a local pop-punk band. She lives outside of Chicago with her husband and daughters. Visit her at www.trishcook.com.

BRENDAN HALPIN is the author of *How Ya Like Me Now*, *Forever Changes*, and *Donorboy*, an Alex Award winner. He has been featured on the *Today* show, NPR's *Fresh Air*, and *Rosie*, as well as in *Good Housekeeping*, the *New York Times* Modern Love column, and several other prominent magazines and newspapers. He lives in Boston with his wife, Suzanne, their three children, and their dog. Visit him at www.brendanhalpin.com.